JACQUELINE WILSON'S
BISCUIT BARREL

Jacqueline Wilson's

Biscuit Barrel

Cliffhanger
and
Buried Alive

Illustrated by Nick Sharratt
and Sue Heap

CORGI YEARLING BOOKS

JACQUELINE WILSON'S BISCUIT BARREL
A CORGI YEARLING : 0 440 86463 1

PRINTING HISTORY
This collection first published in Corgi Yearling 2001
This edition first published 2002

1 3 5 7 9 10 8 6 4 2

Copyright © 2001 by Jacqueline Wilson

CLIFFHANGER
Corgi Yearling edition published 1995

Text copyright © 1995 by Jacqueline Wilson
Illustrations copyright © 1995 by Nick Sharratt

BURIED ALIVE!
Doubleday edition published 1998
Corgi Yearling edition published 1999

Text copyright © 1998 by Jacqueline Wilson
Illustrations copyright © 1998 by Nick Sharratt and Sue Heap

The right of Jacqueline Wilson to be identified as the author of
this work has been asserted in accordance with the Copyright,
Designs and Patents Act 1988

Corgi Yearling Books are published by Random House Children's Books,
61–63 Uxbridge Road, London W5 5SA,
a division of The Random House Group Ltd,
in Australia by Random House Australia (Pty) Ltd,
20 Alfred Street, Milsons Point, Sydney, NSW 2061, Australia,
and in New Zealand by Random House New Zealand Ltd,
18 Poland Road, Glenfield, Auckland 10, New Zealand
and in South Africa by Random House (Pty) Ltd,
Endulini, 5a Jubilee Road, Parktown 2193, South Africa.

Made and printed in Great Britain by
Cox & Wyman Ltd, Reading, Berkshire.

www.kidsatrandomhouse.co.uk

CLIFFHANGER

Jacqueline Wilson

Illustrated by

Nick Sharratt

YEARLING BOOKS

For Tim and Joanna

POST CARD

Dear Mum and Dad
I am at the Adventure Centre.
Well. You know that. You took
me here.
    I have only been here half an
hour. I am not enjoying it so
far. Not one bit.
    With love from
                Tim
    xxxxxxx to Mum
        x to Dad

Mr and Mrs R. Parsons,
10 Rainbow Street,
Didcot,
Oxon

Chapter One

I *knew* I'd hate it. I kept telling and
telling Dad. But he wouldn't listen to
me. He never does.

'I like the sound of this adventure
holiday for children,' said Dad, pointing to the advert in the paper.
'Abseiling, canoeing, archery, mountain biking . . .'

'Sounds a bit dangerous to me,' said
Mum.

I didn't say anything. I went on
watching telly.

'How about it, Tim?' said Dad.
'What about an adventure holiday,
eh?'

'You can't be serious! Tim's much
too young,' said Mum.

I still didn't say anything. I went on

9

Walter Bear

watching telly. But my heart had started thumping under my T-shirt.

'He's nine, for goodness sake!' said Dad.

'But he's young for his age,' said Mum.

I still didn't say anything. I went on watching telly. I stared hard at the screen, wishing there was some way I could step inside.

'Tim?' said Dad.

I didn't look round quickly enough.

'Tim! Stop watching television!' Dad shouted.

I jumped.

'Don't shout at him like that,' said Mum.

'I'm not shouting,' Dad shouted. He took a deep breath. He turned his lips up into a big smile. 'Now, Tim – you'd like to go on an adventure holiday, wouldn't you?'

'He'd hate it,' said Mum.

'Let him answer for himself,' said Dad. He had hold of me by the shoulders.

'I – I don't really like adventures much, Dad,' I said.

Dad went on smiling, but I think he wanted to give my shoulders a shake.

'Well, what do you like, Tim?' asked Dad.

'Watching telly,' I said.

Dad snorted.

'And drawing and reading and doing puzzles,' said Mum. 'And he comes top in all his lessons at school. Apart from games. You know he's hopeless at sport.'

'Only because he doesn't give it a try,' said Dad. 'I was Captain of football and cricket when I was a boy.'

Dad had tried to teach me football. Dad had tried to teach me cricket.

He had tried. And I had tried. But it hadn't worked.

'Tim can't help being bad at games,' said Mum, pulling me away from Dad.

She gave me a cuddle.

'It's because you've turned him into a right Mummy's boy,' said Dad. 'I think an adventure holiday would do him the world of good.'

He wouldn't listen to Mum. He wouldn't listen to me. He booked the adventure holiday.

'You'll love it when you get there,' said Dad. Over and over again.

He bought me new jeans and T-shirts and trainers and a stiff soldier's jacket to make me look tough.

Mum bought me a special safety helmet to wear all the time to keep me safe.

I didn't feel tough. I didn't feel safe.

I needed to hug Walter Bear very hard when Dad drove us to the Adventure Centre. Dad said I shouldn't take a teddy bear with me because the other kids might laugh at me. Mum said I couldn't get to sleep without Walter Bear. I didn't say anything. I hugged Walter even harder, sniffing in his sweet dusty smell.

Dad looked in his driving mirror and saw what I was doing.

'Tim!' said Dad, turning round to frown at me. 'Come on, you're doing it deliberately. Put that silly bear *down*. You'll be sucking your thumb next.'

He was watching me, not watching the road. An old banger suddenly overtook us, making Dad swerve.

'Idiots!' Dad shouted, peeping his horn.

A girl leaned out the open window of the car and yelled right back.

'Slowpokes!' she shouted, and pulled a silly face.

'I hope that girl's not going on the adventure holiday,' said Mum.

I hoped she wasn't going on the

Walter Bear

adventure holiday too. I wished *I* wasn't going on the adventure holiday.

'Look, Tim! I think that's it,' Dad said excitedly.

I didn't look. I shut my eyes tight. I hoped if I wished hard enough I'd somehow whizz through space and end up safe at home. But Dad was already parking the car. Mum kept going on at me, asking why I had my eyes shut and did I feel sick, and I couldn't concentrate hard enough on my wishing. Then Dad opened the car door and yanked me out and hissed at me to stop messing about and say hello to the lady.

'Hello! You must be Tim. I'm Sally. I'm in charge of the Adventure Centre,' she said.

She smiled at me. Dad prodded me

Walter Bear

in the back to make me say hello.

The slowpoke girl was dashing about showing off.

'Now you behave yourself, Kelly,' said her mum, but she didn't sound a bit fierce. She sounded friendly.

Kelly just laughed at her and gave her a hug.

'You can clear off now, Mum,' she said. 'Bye.'

'I think we should make ourselves scarce too,' said Dad. 'Cheerio, Tim.' He bent down and whispered in my ear. 'Now you're really going to try to be a big boy, not a silly baby, eh?'

I didn't say anything. Dad chucked me under the chin.

'You'll have a great time,' said Dad.

'But if you really don't like it then phone and we'll come and get you straight away,' said Mum. 'And write me lots of postcards too. One every day?'

She gave me a hug and a very wet kiss. I wriggled. I was sure Kelly was watching and laughing at me.

'Mum! I'll be OK. Honestly,' I said.

Though I didn't *feel* OK. It was awful seeing them get back in the car without me. I waved like crazy. There was someone on the back seat waving back. Walter Bear! I'd left him in the car!

'Come on then, Tim,' said Sally, putting her arm round my shoulders. 'Hey, Kelly, wait for us.'

Kelly had gone charging through the doors and down the hall of the Adventure Centre.

'Where's all the other children then?' she shouted. 'When are we going to start the adventures, eh? Can I go canoeing first? No, wait a minute, what's that thing called when you dangle down a cliff?'

'Abseiling,' said Sally.

I muttered the words 'dangle' and 'cliff' and felt sick.

'I'm going to love abseiling,' said Kelly, and she threw down her bag and started miming it, rushing backwards.

Walter Bear

She rushed backwards into me, nearly knocking me over.

'Simmer down, Kelly,' said Sally.

'I'm not very good at simmering,' said Kelly, laughing. 'I generally bubble over.'

'So I see!' said Sally, shaking her head. 'OK, you'd both better get unpacked. Your bedrooms are up the stairs at the end. Girls on the right, boys on the left. You'll see a Tiger poster on the doors.'

Kelly and I went up the stairs together. I didn't know what to say to her. I felt silly and shy. She pulled another funny face.

'What did Sally say? Girls to the left? So you go thataway,' said Kelly, giving me a little push to the door on the right.

I was sure she'd got it wrong but Kelly isn't the sort of girl you argue

Walter Bear

with. So I knocked on the right-hand door and then peeped round.

Two girls stared at me, outraged. They were trying on each other's clothes.

'No boys allowed in here!' said the pretty one, tossing her long hair. 'Clear off.'

'Yes, clear off, you,' said her friend.

I cleared off rapidly.

Kelly was being shouted at too. She didn't seem to care.

'Oh oh! Swopsies,' she said, shrugging cheerfully.

I tried the left-hand door this time. Inside, there were two boys messing about with their bags.

'Hello, I'm Giles,' said the taller one. His voice was very posh and he acted very pushy. 'You're going to be in our team. The Tigers. What are you good at then?'

I thought hard.

'Um. Well, I'm OK at Maths and . . .'

'*Games*, you berk!' said Giles, sneering. 'What school teams are you in?'

'I'm not,' I said.

'You're not in *anything*? Oh great!' said Giles sarcastically. 'We've got three girls, old Fatso here, and *you*.'

The fat boy was sprawling on his bed, eating a biscuit.

'Less of the Fatso, *Piles*,' he said, munching.

I giggled. I know what piles are. My dad had them once.

The fat boy giggled too. 'Hi, I'm Biscuits,' he said. 'What's your name, then?'

'Tim,' I said, putting my bag down on the bed next to Biscuits.

'Not *that* one! That's my bed,' said Giles, knocking my bag on to the floor.

'Your bed's that one over there,' said Biscuits. 'We're supposed to get unpacked. They're going to ring a bell when it's teatime. I can't wait, I'm starving.'

He unwrapped another biscuit and started serious munching again. Giles unzipped a tennis racquet and started swinging it wildly in the air, practising his serve.

I started unpacking all my stuff. My T-shirts and pyjamas smelt all clean and flowery of home. I had to bend over my bag so that Giles and Biscuits wouldn't see my watery eyes.

Then I felt a sudden bang on the head.

'Watch out!' I squeaked.

'Sorry. Just practising,' said Giles. 'Oh goodness, you're not blubbing, are you? I hardly touched you.'

I sniffed hard.

'Have you brought your tennis racquet then?' Giles asked.

I started to worry some more.

'I thought they were meant to provide all the racquets and that,' I said.

'That's right,' said Biscuits. He quietly passed me a tissue. It was a bit chocolatey but it was still fine for mopping operations.

'It'll be just ropey old stuff,' said Giles scornfully. 'I've brought my own equipment.'

He started rifling through his bags, showing us. It all looked brand new and very expensive.

'I've brought my own equipment too,' said Biscuits, grinning. He nudged me and pulled open a big picnic bag. I saw bags and bags of biscuits, crisps, apples, sweets and cans of cola.

'Yummy,' I said.

Biscuits rubbed his tummy.

Giles sighed in a superior manner.

'I've brought one bit of equipment,'

Walter Bear

I said, showing him my safety helmet.

I knew it was a mistake as soon as I'd got it out. Especially as Mum had painted TIM in bright pink letters on the front.

Giles did a deliberate double-take.

'What's that, then?' he said. Though of course he knew.

'Well. It's a safety helmet,' I said.

'I see,' said Giles. 'When are you going to wear it then?'

'When I'm . . . when . . .' my voice tailed away.

Giles was serving madly and I had to dodge sharpish.

'When little baby diddums is playing tennis?' Giles jeered. 'In case he gets banged on the bonce, is that it?'

I pretended to ignore him. I wanted to keep well out of Giles's way so I went over to the wardrobe and put all my stuff away. Then I hunched up on my bed and wrote my first postcard.

Biscuits offered me a bite of his biscuit while I was writing it. The biscuit was a bit slurpy and soggy, but it was still nice of him.

I added a P.S. to my first postcard.

P.S. But I have got a friend called Biscuits.

POST CARD

Dear Mum and Dad
I am having a
Truly Terrible Time.
WHY won't you come and
take me home ??????

With love from
Tim

Mr and Mrs R. Parsons,
10 Rainbow Street,
Didcot,
Oxon

Chapter Two

That first evening at the Adventure Centre was awful. Awful awful awful.

Well. Tea was OK. We had beef-burgers and chips and peas. There was tomato sauce on the table. Biscuits and I messed about, pretending the tomato sauce was blood. The pretend started to get a bit real and I stared at the scarlet pool all over my plate and decided I wasn't really hungry any more.

It didn't matter though. Biscuits ate my tea as well as his own.

We sat with Giles. Kelly came and squashed in beside us too. She said hi to me. Giles thought she was my girl-friend!!!

Jake came and talked to us at tea. Jake was our Special Helper. He was tall and sporty and good-looking. All the girls were crazy about him because he looked like some pop star.

I thought he might be a bit bossy and big-headed, but he talked to me just like a friend. I didn't want to be in any stupid team but if I *had* to be in a team then I was very glad it was Jake's team. The Tigers.

G-r-r-r-r-r-r-r-r-r-r-r-r-r-r-r-r-r-r-r-r-r-r-r-r-r.

That's the Tiger Grand Roar.

There were six of us. Giles and Biscuits and me. And Kelly. And Laura and Lesley. They were the girls in Kelly's bedroom. She said they weren't much fun. They just went whisper whisper, giggle giggle. They left Kelly out of things. But she didn't care. Kelly's the sort of girl who doesn't care about anything.

She doesn't even mind if people think her a *baby*. She had this little Troll doll with purple hair. Kelly made the little Troll 'talk' in a tiny voice.

I often make Walter Bear talk to me. His voice is quite growly. But friendly.

I wished and wished I had Walter with me at the Adventure Centre.

The Tigers had to help clear up after tea. We were on kitchen duties. We all moaned because we got lumbered. The Lions didn't have to clear up. Or the Panthers. Or the Cheetahs.

Kelly said she wanted to be a Cheetah and then she could cheat.

Biscuits said he wanted to be a Lion and then he could lie.

So *I* said I wanted to be a Panther so I could pant. And I made funny panting noises. Biscuits laughed and started panting too. So did Kelly. And even Giles joined in.

Laura and Lesley thought we'd all gone nuts.

I started to wonder if it might be fun to be on an adventure holiday. But *then* we all had to go outside and play these terrible games.

I hate games at school.

I hate games in the garden at home.

I hate games on the beach on holiday.

I knew I would hate hate hate games here.

We were all made up with face-paints to look like tigers (orange with black stripes) . . .

or lions (yellow) . . .

or panthers (black) . . .

or cheetahs (beige with black spots).

Laura and Lesley mucked about with the face-paints, making themselves look like grown-up ladies.

Giles made a fuss at first, saying he didn't want his face painted because it was stupid and cissy.

I didn't mind having my face painted. Though it tickled a bit. But I minded terribly when Jake and Sally and the others started setting up posts and handing out balls and bats.

It was a new game. Triangles. A bit like Rounders. We play Rounders at school. I hate it. I'm useless.

'I can't catch,' I said privately to Biscuits.

'I can't flipping *run*,' said Biscuits.

'I can run, I can catch,' said Kelly.

She wanted to be the bowler and so did Giles so there was an argument. Jake said *he* was the bowler. They had to be fielders. And he picked Laura and Lesley and me to man the posts.

Laura and Lesley giggled.

'*Wo*man the posts,' they said.

I didn't say anything at all at first. I was too worried. Especially when Jake told me to be first post.

I swallowed hard.

'Excuse me, Jake,' I squeaked.

'Yes, Tim?'

'I – I don't want to be first post.'

'Why's that, eh?' said Jake.

'I can't catch,' I explained.

'Well, just do your best,' said Jake.

Giles was sighing and looking impatient.

'*I'd* better be first post,' he said.

'No, we'll give Tim a go,' said Jake. 'We're going to keep changing round anyway. Come on, let's get cracking.'

Jake bowled to the first Lion batter. They gave it a tap and then started running. Laura grabbed the ball and threw it to me.

'Here, Tim, catch!' she shouted.

I tried.

I really did.

Dad always yells at me to watch the ball.

I watched it go sailing past my cupped hands.

'He's missed it!' Giles yelled.

'Tim!' said Laura.

'Tim!' said Lesley.

'Tim!' said Kelly.

'Never mind, Tim,' said Jake. 'Next time, eh?'

I hoped and hoped and hoped I might do better next time.

I didn't.

Or the next time.

Or the next.

Or the next.

Or the next.

It was so awful. No-one else was as useless as me.

Biscuits couldn't run very fast at all but he was good at catching and he could hit hard too.

I couldn't hit hard when it was our turn to bat.

I couldn't hit the ball at all.

I was the worst at games. They all started shouting at me. Teasing me. Saying stuff.

When the games were over at last I ran into the Centre and had a bit of a cry by myself locked in the toilets. Then I remembered the phone in the hall.

I didn't have any change on me but I reversed the charges. I got through to Mum.

I started telling her how awful it was and I asked her to come right that minute. She said she would but then Dad started talking too. He kept asking me *why* it was so awful. So I said about them all shouting at me. And Dad said I was making a fuss about nothing. I said I still wanted them to come and get me like they promised. *But you can't always trust your parents.*

Especially your dad.

He said I should see how I felt tomorrow. He wasn't going to come and fetch me tonight. No matter what.

'But you said you'd come and get me if I didn't like it,' I said. 'I don't want to see how I feel tomorrow. It's not *fair*. I didn't want to come here in the first place.'

I was in the middle of saying all this – and a bit more – when Biscuits came along the hall and sort of hovered. So I sniffed a lot and said I'd phone again tomorrow.

'You OK?' said Biscuits as I put the phone down.

I nodded and blew my nose.

Biscuits looked bigger than ever, his sweatshirt straining. He saw me staring.

'Want to see what I've got?' he said, patting his much vaster tummy.

He suddenly gave birth to a big tin of golden syrup.

I laughed, even though I was still a bit snuffly.

Biscuits prized the lid open and stuck in his finger. He licked appreciatively.

'Yum yum yum. Here.' He held out the tin. 'You can share it if you like.'

We were very sticky indeed by bed-time. I wished we didn't have to share a room with Giles. It would have been great if it had just been Biscuits and me. But Giles kept going on and on about how hopeless we were at games and how Mega-Great he was at absolutely everything.

He insisted on demonstrating too. Especially his judo. He had me in this armlock that was horribly painful but Biscuits started waddling round the bedroom in his underpants, flexing his muscles.

'*I* do sumo wrestling, right?' he said, beating his chest. 'So *you'd* bet-ter watch your step, Piles.'

'You look more like a gorilla than a wrestler,' said Giles, but he let go of me.

Biscuits did a *wondrous* gorilla impersonation, making very loud gorilla noises.

I did a gorilla impersonation too.

Giles joined in.

We were all three strutting about and thumping our chests, bellowing, when Jake came barging into the bedroom.

'Hey, hey! Calm down, you lot. You're like a lot of monkeys at a zoo,' said Jake.

'Exactly!' I said.

'Hum hum. Me want banana,' said Biscuits, still being a gorilla.

'You're going to explode one day, Biscuits,' said Jake. 'Come on, into bed, you lot.'

'What are we doing tomorrow, Jake?' Giles asked.

'We're going for a bit of a climb – and then it's abseiling,' said Jake.

'Great!' said Giles, jumping up and down.

'*Not* so great,' said Biscuits, pretending to pass out on to his bed.

'Utterly ungreat,' I said.

My heart had started thumping again. Jake saw my face.

'It *is* great, fellows, really,' said Jake. 'Come on, lie down now.'

'Just got to get something,' said Giles, haring over to his bag.

He dug deep . . . and came out with a teddy bear. Giles's bear had a stitched nose stuck right up in the air and a sneery mouth.

'Old teddy, eh?' said Jake.

'He's not any old teddy, he's Sir Algernon Honeypot,' said Giles.

'Well, settle down with his sirship, then,' said Jake.

Biscuits was rootling about in his bag now.

'Biscuits! No more food, do you hear me?' said Jake.

'I'm just getting Dog Hog,' said Biscuits.

'Who?' said Jake.

Biscuits produced a long browny-pink knitted creature with floppy limbs and a curly tail. Biscuits made it prance about his bed.

'We can't work out if he's a dog or a pig. My granny knitted him and she's not very great at knitting actually,' said Biscuits.

Jake looked at me.

'Have you got your teddy, Tim?'

I just shook my head. I couldn't say a thing.

I got into bed and pulled the sheets over my head. My arms felt so *empty* without Walter. And no-one would have laughed at me or called me a baby for having a cuddly toy.

I wanted my Walter Bear *so* much.

I don't know when I went to sleep.

I kept waking up in the night.

And then it was suddenly day, and Jake was in our bedroom again, telling us to rise and shine. We were going up in the hills straight after breakfast.

Abseiling!

Chapter Three

It took ages and ages to get up to the top of the hill. And all the way up I kept thinking about what it would be like coming *down*.

The others raced ahead, desperate to get there first.

I was jolly determined to be last.

Jake kept yelling to Biscuits and me to hurry up. We went as slowly as possible. And then even slower. And then we slowed almost to a standstill.

'Come *on*, you guys! We're all waiting!' Jake shouted.

He had the others gathered round ready to learn about abseiling. Biscuits and I had to gather too, puffing and panting.

It was like being on the edge of the world. I took one look at the steep drop and started shaking. Kelly and Giles were pushing and shoving each other, arguing about who had got to the top first. They didn't even seem to notice that if they took six steps the wrong way they'd be pushing and shoving in thin air.

'Hey, hey! No messing around now,' said Jake. 'This is the serious bit. OK. Abseiling for beginners!'

He got all the ropes out of his backpack.

'Who's going to go first?'

'Me! Me!' said Giles.

'No, me! Pick me, Jake. *Please*,' said Kelly.

'You two are always first,' said Jake.

He put his arm round Laura and

40

Lesley, who were hanging on to each other.

'How about you, Laura? Or Lesley?' said Jake.

'Lesley can go first,' said Laura.

'No, *you* can go first, Laura,' said Lesley.

Jake laughed. Then he looked at me.

'How about you, Tim?'

'No!' I squeaked.

Biscuits suddenly stepped forward. 'I'll have a go,' he said.

We all stared at him, stunned.

'Great!' said Jake, giving him a pat on the back. 'OK. Come and step into the harness, Biscuits.'

'That's going to be a bit of a squeeze!' said Giles.

'Why do the boys always go first? It's not fair,' said Kelly.

'You lot pipe down,' said Jake. 'Watch carefully and listen.' He was helping Biscuits get the ropes sorted around him. 'We'll hitch this up and tighten it . . .'

'It's tight already,' said Giles.

'Giles! Shut it!' said Jake. 'Now, we tie up all the buckles and clip this gadget here – tighten it up, see, so it can't be opened. That means you can't fall out.'

'Are you sure?' said Biscuits.

He was starting to sound as if he was regretting his decision. He shifted from one foot to the other, helplessly trussed up like a turkey.

'I'm one hundred per cent certain, pal,' said Jake. 'Now, you go down at your own pace —'

Biscuits screwed up his face.

'What if I get dizzy?'

'Any time you want to stop you just pull the ropes apart. OK? Now, I'll just secure myself, right. And then we're ready for your big moment, Biscuits.'

'Good luck, Biscuits. I think you're a hero,' I said earnestly.

Biscuits beamed at me – though his teeth had started chattering.

'OK. Start walking backwards

towards the edge, Biscuits,' said Jake.

'Er. This is when it starts to get a bit . . .' Biscuits wavered.

Even Giles and Kelly looked relieved that they weren't going first now. The thought of stepping backwards into space made my legs tremble inside my tracksuit.

'You'll be fine, I promise,' said Jake. 'When you get to the edge stick your bottom out, legs and feet at right angles to the cliff – and don't let go of the rope! Especially not with your left hand. You walk yourself down. You're in control. Your bodyweight helps you down.'

'Then Biscuits' bodyweight is going to whizz him down mega-fast,' said Kelly.

'Shut up, Kelly,' said Jake. 'Come on, Biscuits. Over you go. I'll buy you a chocky biscuit for going first, OK?'

'How about a huge great *bag* of biscuits?' said Biscuits.

He started shuffling backwards to the edge – and then – OVER IT!

'That's it. Good boy!' said Jake. 'Don't let go with your right hand. Down you go. Easy does it. Great. Absolutely perfect! One foot after the other. Are you watching, kids? Biscuits is doing a grand job.'

I couldn't watch. But everyone suddenly cheered – which meant Biscuits had made it right to the bottom of the cliff.

I didn't dare look all the way down but I shouted 'Well done, Biscuits,' into the wind.

'There! I told you it was easy,' said Jake, hauling the ropes and harness back after Biscuits had unscrewed himself. 'OK, Tim. You next.'

'No!'

'Yes,' said Jake, coming over to me.

'No,' I said.

'You've all got to go sooner or later,' said Jake.

'Later,' I insisted.

'No. Sooner,' said Jake. 'Get it over with.'

'I can't,' I said.

'Yes you can, Tim,' said Jake, holding my hand.

'He's scared,' said Giles.

'We all get scared,' said Jake. 'Especially the first time.' He bent down and looked me straight in the eye. 'But you'll see it's easy, Tim. Trust me. Now. Into the harness.'

I found I was being strapped in before I could get away. Jake was telling me things about this rope in this hand, that rope in that, but the wind was whipping his words away. I couldn't listen properly anyway. There was just this roaring inside my head.

'Don't let go of the rope, right?' said Jake.

I felt as if my head was going to burst right out of my personalized safety helmet.

This couldn't be real. It couldn't be happening to me. If I closed my eyes maybe it would all turn into a nightmare and then I'd wake up in bed at home with Walter Bear.

'Tim?' said Jake. 'Open your eyes! Now, your pal Biscuits is down there waiting for you. Come on. Start backing towards the edge.'

I backed one step. Then another. Then I stopped.

'I can't!'

'Yes you can,' said Jake. 'You'll see. Over you go. Don't worry. You can't fall. You just have to remember, you *don't* let go of the rope.'

I stared at him and started backing some more. Then my heels suddenly lost contact with the ground. I slipped backwards and suddenly . . . there I was! Suspended. In mid-air.

'*Help!*'

I reached forward, desperate.

I had to hang on to something.

I grabbed at the rock.

I let go of the rope!

Suddenly I was sliding backwards, backwards, backwards.

I screamed.

I caught hold of the rock, though my fingers bent right back. I clung to it, sobbing.

I heard them shouting up above me.

'He's fallen!'

'He's let go of the rope.'

'I *knew* he would!'

'Trust Tim to blow it.'

'He's *stuck*.'

'Don't stop, Tim!' Biscuits called from underneath me.

I turned my head and tried to look at him. The whole world started swerving and swooping. Biscuits seemed a tiny blob millions and millions of miles below me. I was hanging by my hands in whirling space.

'Help!'

'It's OK, Tim. Don't panic,' Jake called down.

'Don't panic, Tim, don't panic!' Kelly yelled. 'He's panicking, isn't he, Jake?'

'Sh, Kelly. All of you. Just back off, eh?' Jake said. 'Now. Tim. Listen. You've let go of the rope.'

'I know!'

'But it's OK. You can't fall. You're safe, I promise.'

'I don't feel safe. I feel *sick*.'

'Well, you can get yourself down in a couple of ticks. All you need to do is grab hold of the rope.'

'How???'

'Just let go of the rock and —'

'I can't!' Was Jake crazy? The rock was the only thing stopping me swinging through space. I *couldn't* let go.

'You're safely strapped into your harness,' Jake called. 'You don't need to clutch the rock. You've just got to take hold of the rope and then you're back in business. See the rope? Tim! Open your eyes!'

'I can't look down.'

'Look up. At me,' said Jake.

I tilted my head and dared peep out between my eyelashes. Jake was leaning right over the edge, not too terribly far away. He gave me a thumbs-up sign.

'That's the ticket. Now. It's OK. Have a little rest if you like. It's not so bad now, is it?'

'Yes!'

'You can dangle there all day if you really want,' said Jake.

'No!'

'Or you can get hold of that old rope and walk yourself down, one foot at a time, easy-peasy. Mmm?'

I peered up at him.

'Can't you pull me up?' I begged.

'We're trying to get you down, pal, not up!' said Jake. 'You can do it. You're being ever so brave.'

He had to be joking!

'Stay there long enough and you'll get such a head for heights you'll become a trapeze artist,' said Jake.

'I don't think!'

'So just reach out —' Jake urged.

I thought about it. My fingers were hurting terribly. My hands were so scratched and sore. I *couldn't* hang there for ever. Maybe if I let go and grabbed the rope I *could* get down. So I loosened my grip, I reached out suddenly, I tried to grab . . .

I swung round and it was so scary I shut my eyes and caught hold of the rock all over again.

I heard the others groaning. But Jake didn't give up on me.

'Nearly. Try again. Go on.'

So I tried again. I reached out. I

50

made another grab at the rope. My hand was sticky with sweat but I got it – I held on to it – I had it safe!

'Well done!' Jake called. 'There! I knew you could. Just keep hanging on to it this time, eh? Now walk yourself down. One step.'

I tried to move my feet. They were numb inside my boots. I made a teeny-tiny mouse-move downwards.

'Great!' said Jake. 'Now another step.'

My other leg moved. And I moved too. I was going down.

'We're back in business,' said Jake. 'There we go. That's it. You're getting the hang of it now.'

'I'm doing it!' I said, stepping myself down through space.

'That's right. You're doing it, Tim,' Jake called. 'You're nearly halfway down. Doing just great. Carry on. Nice and easy. Good boy. Well done.'

'I'm doing it,' I mumbled. 'I'm doing it. I'm doing it. It's awful. But I'm doing it!'

'Come on, Tim!' Biscuits called up at me. He sounded much nearer now. 'You're nearly there!'

I carried on, quicker and quicker – and then suddenly I was at the bottom and Biscuits gave me such a thump on the back to congratulate me that I very nearly fell over.

'You did it, you did it, you did it!' Biscuits sang.

Jake was cheering me from right up at the top of the rock.

'Well done, Tim! It wasn't so bad, was it? Do you want another go, eh?'

I shook my head so hard my helmet wobbled.

'Never ever *ever* again!'

All the others managed it without making a fuss. Giles was especially good at it. I knew he would be.

He went on and on and on at me going back to the Centre.

'You were so *scared*!' he said. 'You just dangled there. And you *cried*! Boo hoo, boo hoo, little baby.'

He kept pushing and punching me too, when he thought Jake wasn't watching. Really hard.

After tea Jake asked me to help him look for lost balls in the garden. Just him and me.

I found a red ball right in the middle of the roses. Jake was pleased with me.

'Well done, Tim.' He patted me on the back. His hand stayed on my shoulder. 'You're finding it a bit tough at the moment, aren't you, Tim?'

'They keep teasing me, saying I'm scared. Well, it's mostly one person in particular. In my bedroom. The one who isn't Biscuits.'

Jake sat down and I did too.

'Giles?' said Jake, throwing the red ball at me.

'Giles!' I said, sighing, catching the ball.

'You caught it!' said Jake.

I threw the ball back. He threw it to me. I caught it each time. But Jake was giving me very easy throws.

'You could try standing up to him,' Jake said, bouncing the ball.

'Hmm!' The ball skidded into the roses again and I went to fetch it. I found a little wiggly worm too. It almost got run over by the ball, but not quite. I stroked it very gently.

'I'm like this little worm,' I said, holding it in my hand. 'And Giles is like a great big blackbird. Going peck peck peck at me.'

Jake seemed surprised that I liked worms so I told him about this pet worm I had once called William. I filled a shoe-box with earth and made him a special Wormotel but then Mum made a fuss and I had to empty the shoe-box into the garden – and William got emptied out too.

'I'll tell you a secret, Tim,' said Jake.

Jake said he was scared of worms! Always, ever since he was a little boy. And all the other boys teased him and threw worms at him to make him squeal.

'So one day I thought this is nuts. I made myself pick up a worm and I threw it right back. And it was OK after that.'

I wondered whether Giles was scared of worms.

Jake said everyone's scared of something. Mice. The dark. Wetting the bed!

I held the wiggly worm out and he squealed and made out he was dead scared. But he was only kidding.

'I think you've been kidding all along, Jake,' I said. 'To make me feel better.'

Jake laughed and said I was amazing at sussing things out.

I've sussed out one thing. I know what my friend Biscuits is scared of. Running out of biscuits!

POST CARD

Dear Mum and Dad
I went abseiling!!!
I didn't like it. (Understatement of the century.) I let go of the rope and was in MORTAL DANGER. But I managed to grab it again. I survived. Just.

With love from
Tim

P.S. It's canoeing today. I could still drown.

Mr and Mrs R. Parsons,
10 Rainbow Street,
Didcot,
Oxon

Chapter Four

Biscuits and I teamed up for the canoe race. Biscuits sat at the front. Our canoe tipped forwards. We swopped round which was *exceedingly* difficult. We got a bit wet in the process, but eventually I was squashed in the front and Biscuits sat behind me. Our canoe tilted backwards. We decided to put up with it. We agreed not to take the canoe race too seriously.

Giles and Kelly took it very seriously indeed. Jake had paired them up in one canoe. Giles stuck his nose in the air at the thought of sharing with Kelly. Kelly *held* her nose at the thought of sharing with Giles. But they made a very speedy pair

Theresa

and they were soon racing ahead through the water. Laura and Lesley were nippy too, paddling away like crazy.

'Come *on,* you Tigers!' Giles yelled, craning back at us.

There were just two huge Panthers ahead of Giles and Kelly. They had arm muscles like cannon balls and were way out in front. Giles and Kelly paddled frantically, desperate to catch them up.

'Nutters!' said Biscuits, wiping his brow. 'Phew! I don't think much of this canoeing lark, do you, Tim?'

'Yeah. This isn't my idea of fun,' I said, paddling hard.

'You can say that again,' said Biscuits.

'This isn't my idea of fun,' I said.

'You can say that again,' said Biscuits.

'This isn't my idea of fun,' I said, cracking up laughing.

'You can say that again,' said Biscuits, spluttering.

We were soon laughing so much we nearly capsized our canoe.

Giles and Kelly were getting nearer and nearer the mighty Panthers. They drew close, maybe too close. The Panthers went a bit wobbly – and suddenly Giles and Kelly were ahead.

'We're in front!' Giles yelled triumphantly.

'We are the champions!' Kelly sang, and she took something small out of her pocket and gave a victory wave.

She waved a little too vigorously. The small something flew through the air and did a swallow dive into the river.

Kelly screamed.

'Theresa! Come back! You can't swim!' She sounded frantic.

Giles was growing frantic too. He was shouting at Kelly.

'Sit down! You'll have us over. What are you *doing*?'

Kelly twisted and turned, practically paddling backwards.

'What's up with Kelly?' asked Biscuits, blinking at her.

'She's dropped Theresa in the water. You know. Her little Troll doll,' I explained.

We knew all about Kelly's lucky mascot. Jake and Sally didn't.

They heard Kelly yelling desperately and came whizzing over in their own canoe.

'Theresa's drowning!' Kelly sobbed.

'*Where?* Which canoe? There isn't a Theresa on the course! Kelly, *who's* Theresa?' they shouted urgently, Jake jumping up to dive to the rescue.

'She's her stupid Troll doll,' Giles said disgustedly, as the mighty Panthers raced past towards the winning post.

Jake sat down again, and he and

Sally waved their hands and went Phew!

'*Please*, Jake! Can't you dive in and look for her?' Kelly yelled. 'Oh, Theresa. Where *are* you?'

'Hey!' said Biscuits, his eyes beady. 'Look, Theresa's just bobbing past!'

I looked – and saw a little purple blob floating off towards the bank.

'It *is* Theresa! It's OK, Kelly,' I shouted. 'We've spotted her, Biscuits and me. We'll get her.'

'Yeah, we'll get her out for you, Kelly,' said Biscuits. 'Er . . . how do we get the canoe to go sideways, Tim?'

'Like this? Mmm. No. Like *this*?'

Our canoe wobbled dramatically as we experimented.

'What are you two playing at?' Giles yelled. 'Finish the race first. We've all got to finish or we won't get any

Theresa

points. You can go back for her doll afterwards.'

'She can't wait!' said Kelly.

'Come on, Biscuits,' I said. 'Before she gets swallowed up by a fish or something.'

We made for the bank as best we could.

'You berks!' Giles yelled in disgust. 'You weedy nerdy little cissies.'

'I wish *he'd* get swallowed up by a fish,' said Biscuits. 'A socking great shark.'

'He's going to get us later,' I said.

'Oh, pooh,' said Biscuits. 'We'll get *him.*'

'To the rescue. Super-Tim and Biscuit-Boy!'

'*Dan-de-dan-dan-daaaan,*' Biscuits chanted.

We reached the bank. Theresa was

Theresa

bobbing in the scummy shallows, her purple hair wafting like water-weed. I got my paddle and used it like a fish slice, scooping Theresa up in the air.

She had never been a very pretty little doll. She'd now lost whatever looks she'd had. But Kelly was still thrilled to get her back. She hugged and kissed her. And you'll never guess what. She hugged and kissed *me*.

Biscuits said he was very glad that *I* was the one who fished her out.

When we were in the kitchens clearing up after tea, Kelly tried to tame Theresa's alarming new hair-style with a small scrubbing-brush.

Laura and Lesley sighed.

'You're hopeless, Kelly,' said Laura. 'Look, give her here, I'll do it.'

She had her own little pocket hair-brush. Kelly held Theresa while Laura brushed and styled her purple tresses.

'You're ever so good at hairstyles, Laura,' said Lesley.

'Keep Theresa *still*, Kelly,' said Laura.

'She's shivering,' said Kelly. She peered round and found a scrunched-up J-cloth. 'Here. This will keep you warm until we get your little dress dry.'

'Look, I could do with that cloth, Kelly,' said Giles, washing dishes at the sink. 'This one's all holey and horrible.'

'Theresa's need is greater than yours, Giles,' said Kelly firmly.

'You and that stupid doll.'

'She's *not* a doll, she's a *troll*,' said Kelly.

'We were winning,' Giles wailed. 'And yet we ended up last because of you and Biscuits and *Tim*.'

He dug me hard with his elbow, right in my tummy. 'Why did you have to mess about for hours getting Kelly's stupid doll?'

'TROLL!' Kelly shouted, flicking washing-up water in Giles's face.

'Kelly! Cut it out,' said Giles,

splashing her back. He splashed me too. 'And then you got your canoe stuck in the mud on the bank!'

'It wasn't our fault,' said Biscuits, emerging from the food cupboard, his hand deep in a packet of Frosties.

'Yes, it's not *our* fault we're not very good at canoeing,' I said.

'The thing is, Tim, you're not good at *anything*,' said Giles.

Kelly splashed Giles again.

Giles splashed Kelly. He also splashed Laura by mistake.

'Giles!' Laura squeaked. 'Look at my shirt, it's soaking!'

'Oh, Giles, you've got Laura all wet,' said Lesley.

'Tim's the one that's wet,' said Giles, splashing me again. 'Wet and weedy and pathetic.'

'You shut up, Piles,' said Biscuits,

flicking Frosties at him. 'You're the one that's pathetic.'

'Yeah, Tim rescued Theresa. He's a hero!' said Kelly, and she splashed Giles.

He splashed her back. Copiously. Laura *and* Lesley got soaked this time. So they splashed Giles back. He splashed me again. Biscuits emptied the Frosties all over him. We all burst out laughing because he looked so funny. I threw my wiping-cloth at him. I missed, but it didn't matter. We all started splashing and shrieking and then Jake suddenly charged into the kitchen and bellowed at us.

'What on *earth* are you lot playing at?'

We ended up on our hands and knees doing an awful lot of mopping.

POST CARD

Dear Mum and Dad

Us Tigers all got into Mega-Trouble last night. But it was good fun all the same. And then Kelly gave me a Kit Kat before we went to bed. I shared it with Biscuits. I had the Kit and he had the Kat. Biscuits is my friend. And Kelly. Even though she's a girl.

With love from

Tim xxxxx

P.S. We're doing the Crazy Bucket race today. Weird! How can you race buckets ????

Mr and Mrs R. Parsons,
10 Rainbow Street,
Didcot,
Oxon

Chapter Five

I found out!

Jake and Sally had set this huge great obstacle race. We were all lined up in our teams: the Lions, the Panthers, the Cheetahs – and us. Giles was dead eager. Kelly was bobbing about, Theresa clutched in her fist. Laura and Lesley were giggling. Biscuits and I were *groaning*.

'It's not my idea of fun,' I whispered.

'You can say that again,' Biscuits whispered back.

We kept this up all the time Sally was explaining what we had to do. It involved a lot of running. Lots and lots of running.

We had to run to the paddling pool

Thirsty baby tiger

and fill our buckets with water and then we had to run – with the full buckets – all the way round the field to the slide and then – still with the buckets – we had to climb up it and slide down and *then* we had to run to the sandpit and stagger across – with the buckets – and THEN we had to run to the stream and at the other side of the water there were four thirsty baby big cats desperate for a bucketful of water. Well, that's what Sally said.

'Can you go through it again, Sally? I wasn't concentrating,' said Biscuits, grinning.

Sally pretended to clip him over the ear.

Giles was dead set on getting the rules right.

'So it's the team that fills the

painted rubbish bin first that wins, yes?'

'They're not bins, Giles, they're babies. A baby lion, a baby panther, a baby cheetah, and *we've* got a baby tiger,' said Kelly. 'Doesn't it look sweet?'

Giles screwed up his face in disgust at this whimsy.

I thought the bins looked good. The Baby Lion bin was painted yellow, the Baby Panther bin was painted black, the Baby Cheetah bin was painted beige with black spots, and our Baby Tiger bin looked the best, painted orange with black stripes. They all had cardboard ears and beady eyes and the swing tops made excellent movable mouths. Jake demonstrated, making them open their mouths to pant for water.

Jake jumped over the stream to get to them. He's got long legs but it was still quite a stretch for him. And he wasn't carrying a bucket of water. But there were four drainpipes across the stream. It looked as if we were in for a very wobbly walk across.

'And the team that fills the bin first wins?' Giles repeated impatiently, raring to go.

'Not so fast, pal,' said Sally. 'The first team gets forty points, the second team gets thirty, the third team gets twenty. The last team only gets ten points.'

'Guess who's going to be last,' I muttered to Biscuits.

'But the Crazy Bucket race isn't just about coming first,' said Sally, smiling. 'We measure how much water is in each of the bins. That's just as important. You get forty points if your bin is the fullest. Then thirty, then twenty, then ten.'

'It's starting to sound like a maths lesson,' said Lesley. 'I can't get the hang of it, can you, Laura?'

'It's all much simpler than it sounds,' said Sally. 'Cheer up. It's fun!'

Biscuits pulled a silly face at me. I

pulled one back. Giles pushed us into place.

'Come on, you lot, stop messing about. We're going to win, right?'

'Wrong!'

'Look, *try*,' said Giles.

'My dad always tells me to try,' I told Biscuits. 'And I do. But it doesn't work.'

'Right everyone,' Sally called. 'Get ready. One. Two. Three. GO!'

We all started running. Guess what. Giles got to the pool first.

'Come *on*, you Tigers!' he bawled as he filled his bucket.

Biscuits and I were nearly last at the pool. We filled our buckets right to the brim. We certainly weren't going to fill our baby big cat bin first, so we knew we had to bring our entire bucketful.

Thirsty baby tiger

It was hard going, running with a full bucket. We had to be ever so careful not to spill any. Some of the faster kids swung their buckets and sprinkled water all down their socks. Biscuits didn't spill any, but he was slower than ever. I jogged along beside him, proud that I hadn't spilled a single drop.

And then one of the Cheetahs pushed past me, his bucket banging hard into my back. I staggered and fell headlong, spilling all the water in my bucket.

'Ooooh!' All the breath was knocked out of me.

'Oh Tim!' said Biscuits, ever so upset. 'That Cheetah pushed into you on purpose. He really *did* cheat!'

Giles was yelling at me from a long way off.

Thirsty baby tiger

'Tim! You're so *useless*!'

I lay there, still juddering. I had my eyes shut because I was trying very hard not to cry.

'You cheaty old Cheetah!' I heard Kelly bellow.

There was a yell and a thump and a splash. When I opened my eyes I saw the Cheetah sprawling on the ground, soaking wet, Kelly standing over him triumphantly.

'Hey! Hey! You'll all end up disqualified if you're not careful!' Jake called. 'Is Tim OK?'

I wasn't sure. There was wet on my knees. It wasn't just the water from my bucket. I was *bleeding*.

'Maybe you'd better go and get them bandaged?' said Biscuits.

I stood up very slowly. The blood spurted a bit more. I had a truly great excuse to get out of finishing the race.

I looked at Biscuits. I looked at Kelly. I looked at Laura and Lesley, who were running back to see if I was all right. I looked at Giles. He was yelling again.

'Come *on*! We've all got to finish. You can't let us down, Tim!'

I didn't mind letting Giles down *at all*. But I didn't want to spoil it for the others.

'I'm OK,' I said. 'I'll run back to fill my bucket again.'

'We'll wait for you,' said Biscuits.

'No, I'll catch you up.'

So I ran all the way back to the pool, even though my knees were hurting quite badly. Then I filled my bucket and started the long run again, way way way behind all the others, though two Lions then bumped into each other and had to go back to the pool as well. And more came a cropper on the slide. There was a whole bunch who fought to go first and spilled all their water. By the time *I* got to the slide it was clear and I could take it slowly. I didn't spill a drop.

I caught Biscuits up at the sandpit. We staggered through the sand,

Thirsty baby tiger

balancing our buckets.

'It's like being at the seaside,' I said.

'I couldn't half do with an ice-cream,' said Biscuits longingly. 'Or an ice-lolly. Or a can of cola. No, a bottle of Tizer. Or an ice-cream soda. No, better, a Knickerbocker Glory . . .'

He was off in a wistful food fantasy right up until we got to the stream. Jake was swinging the bin mouths again.

'They're so *thirsty*,' Jake called. 'They're desperate. Water, water!'

But we were all the other side of the stream with our buckets. None of the others had made it across. Some of the children were very wet, after several attempts.

'Let me have a go,' said Kelly, elbowing Giles and Laura and Lesley out of the way.

She started edging along the

79

Thirsty baby tiger

wobbly drainpipe, holding her bucket out. The drainpipe was only lightly wedged into the ground at either side of the stream. It jiggled at each step. Kelly wobbled, but got halfway across. She turned round to make sure we were all watching her. She wobbled again, lost her balance, slipped off the drainpipe and fell into the stream. She had the presence of mind to clutch her bucket to her chest so that it didn't *all* spill. She added a bit of stream water for luck when she thought Jake wasn't watching.

'Hey, Kelly, no sly refilling that bucket!' he shouted. 'Empty half of that out.'

Kelly sighed and muttered but did as she was told.

'*I'll* have a go,' said Giles. 'I'll have a little practice without my bucket.'

He made it halfway across too.

Then the drainpipe jiggled and Giles wobbled and he went flying too. He made a leap for it so that he didn't get totally soaked like Kelly. He just got water all down his trouser legs.

'You look like you've wet yourself, Giles,' said Laura, and she and Lesley fell about laughing.

'Come on!' Jake urged from the other side of the bank. 'Think of a way to give these babies a proper drink.'

Kelly was peeling her sodden shoes and socks off.

'Hey, why don't we just paddle across?' she said. 'I'm sure it's shallow enough.'

'Not allowed,' said Jake, and he picked up a log and threw it in the stream. 'See that log? It's *really* a crocodile. You paddle, he'll come along and enjoy a leg sandwich.'

'Well, it's easier without shoes and socks on anyway,' said Kelly, having another go across the drainpipe.

She ran to show how easy it was.

She slipped and fell in again.

'Whoops,' said Kelly, clambering up the bank. '*Slightly* easier.' She shook herself like a wet dog and then dug Theresa out of her pocket and gave her a squeeze too. 'We're not too keen on this swimming lark, are we, Theresa?'

'This is stupid,' said Laura. 'It's too difficult, Jake. It's all right for you. You can jump across.'

'I bet *I* could jump across,' said Giles. 'Look. Watch me.'

He took several giant steps backwards, revved up, hurtled forward, leapt into space and soared over the stream. He staggered a bit when he landed in the mud at the other side, but he'd made it. He punched the air triumphantly, thrilled with himself.

'But you haven't got your bucket,' said Kelly.

The Cheetahs were watching. Their tallest boy tried leaping the stream with his bucket. He made it to the other side. But most of the water sprayed out of his bucket as he leapt. Lots of the others had a go. Without success.

'They're s-o-o-o-o-o thirsty, these baby big cats,' said Jake. 'Try harder!'

'We are jolly well trying,' said Kelly.

'Think of a way of giving them their drink,' said Jake.

'Well, we've all tried to get across,' said Kelly. 'Apart from Biscuits and Tim.' She looked at us hopefully.

'You've got to be joking!' Giles called from the other side of the stream. 'If Fatso stands on the drainpipe, he'll bust it in two.'

'I'll bust you in two in a minute, Piles,' said Biscuits.

'Tim?' said Kelly.

'There's even less point asking him,' said Giles.

I was thinking. It was like a puzzle

Thirsty baby tiger

Thirsty baby tiger

game. We were all trying to do it the hard way. There had to be an *easy* way . . .

I suddenly had an idea. Though I wasn't sure if it would be allowed.

'Well,' I started.

But they were all watching one of the Lion girls who had balanced her way right along the drainpipe. She was almost at the end. But then she suddenly wobbled – and went.

'Oooh!' said everyone.

'See. *No-one* can do it, Jake,' said Laura, getting cross.

Jake just laughed at her.

'Did you have an idea, Tim?' he called.

'*He* won't be able to do it,' said Laura. 'He fell over just on the field.'

'You try walking the drainpipe, Laura, I'm sure you could do it,' said Lesley.

'If you can get the bucket three quarters of the way over then I can reach across and get it,' said Giles.

'But you don't have to do it that way,' I said.

'You shut up, Tim,' Giles shouted.

I'd suddenly had enough of being shouted at. And I really did have a good idea.

'No, *you* shut up, Giles,' I yelled. 'Pick your end of the drainpipe up and stick it in the baby tiger's mouth.'

Giles stared at me, going, 'You what?'

But Jake jumped up and down and gave me the thumbs-up sign. I'd cracked it!

'Kelly and Biscuits, you hold the drainpipe this end,' I said, telling them what to do. 'Laura and Lesley, pass me the buckets. Look!'

It was so *simple*. We didn't have to walk across the stream on the drain-pipes. They were hollow inside, like giant straws. We could empty the water down the drainpipe right into the Baby Tiger bin.

And that's exactly what we did.

'Well done, Tim!' Jake shouted.

'Oh, Tim! Brilliant!' said Kelly, giving me a hug. 'You're so clever.'

'Super-Tim,' said Biscuits.

'Why didn't we think of it,' said Laura.

'Look, everyone's copying us now!' said Lesley.

'But *we've* won!' said Giles, capering about. 'We're first to fill the bin – and we've got it nearly full to the top too. We've *won*! Hurray for Tim!'

All the Tigers jumped up and down and cheered. Cheering me. And I jumped up and down and cheered me too!

POST CARD

Dear Mum and Dad
Guess what! We won the bucket race!!!
And it was all because <u>I</u> sussed out
how to do it. Honest. The other Tigers
all think I'm Mega-Brilliant. Even
Giles. Wonders will never cease.
    I can think of another Wonder.
I'm quite enjoying my adventure
holiday now. In fact I almost wish
we weren't going home tomorrow!
        With love from
            Tim
        xxxxx to Mum
        xxxxx to Dad

Mr and Mrs R. Parsons,
10 Rainbow Street,
Didcot,
Oxon

Chapter Six

Time is a funny thing. If you listen to a clock it goes tick tick tick. It doesn't go tick-tick-tick-tick-tick sometimes and t-i-c-k t-i-c-k t-i-c-k other times. And yet the first two days of my adventure holiday went so s-l-o-w-l-y that years and years seemed to go by. But the *last* two days went whizz-whizz-whizz.

You'll never guess which team ended up the over-all winners! We did. The Tigers. Kelly and Giles and Laura and Lesley and Biscuits and me.

We got clapped and cheered by everyone and then Sally and Jake gave us all a prize. We had to put our hands in this big box. I felt something

Biscuits Tiger

furry. We all did. We scrabbled around until we'd all got a handful and then we pulled them out the box. Six toy tigers, baby ones, with big eyes and smiley mouths and soft paddy-paws.

We all laughed and mucked about, making them roar. My tiger is a bit fatter than the others. He seems stuffed to bursting. I've called him Biscuits.

The *real* Biscuits should rename himself Sausages. He ate fourteen and a half sausages at the Camp Cook-Out. (The half was mine. I dropped it in the grass and it got a bit muddy but Biscuits couldn't bear to waste it.) He also ate two burgers and five chicken wings, washed down with three cans of cola. My friend Biscuits has a Mega-Superior Stomach.

He's got a good loud voice too. We all had a Giant Roar competition between the Lions, the Tigers, the Panthers and the Cheetahs.

'Right, us Tigers, let's hear you. ROAR!' Giles yelled, conducting us.

He roared until he was red in the face, but he'd been shouting so much bossing us about that he didn't have much voice left. Laura and Lesley had high voices that weren't loud enough. I wasn't much use either. I tried and tried, but my roars came out small and squeaky. Kelly did much better. She was squashed up beside me and when she opened her mouth and let rip I had to put my hands over my ears. But Biscuits did better. He threw back his head and *bellowed* from the pit of his magnificent stomach.

We won the Giant Roar competition too. I'm *SO* glad I'm a Tiger and not a Lion or a Panther or a Cheetah.

Giles and Biscuits and I stayed awake ever so late, swopping jokes and acting daft. Jake had to come and tell us off three times. But he didn't get really cross. I do like Jake. I do like Biscuits.

I even *almost* liked Giles that last night. And when we were quiet at last and snuggled up to go to sleep it didn't matter that I didn't have Walter Bear. I had little Biscuits Tiger to cuddle instead.

POST CARD

Dear Kelly
    All right. I will be your
boyfriend if you really want.
But if you come and stay
with me and Biscuits is here
then it's a secret, OK?
            love from
                Tim
            xxx

    x to Theresa

Ms Kelly Davis,
102 Tower House,
Tower Road,
Handsworth,
Birmingham

POST CARD

Dear Biscuits-Boy

I wish we were still having Adventures! My dad is ever so chuffed we won. My mum is just glad I'm back safe. She says to ask your mum if you can come and stay. Kelly might be coming too. Has she written to you? She's written to me twice already!

How many biscuits have you consumed since I saw you? Is it A) 10 B) 100 c) 1000 ???

Your pal
Super-Tim

Mr 'Biscuits' Baker,
39 Marlow Road,
Market Harborough,
Leicestershire

BURIED ALIVE!

Jacqueline Wilson

Illustrations by Nick Sharratt
and Sue Heap

CORGI YEARLING BOOKS

Chapter One

To Nicholas
Ted and George
and David and Gary

Chapter One

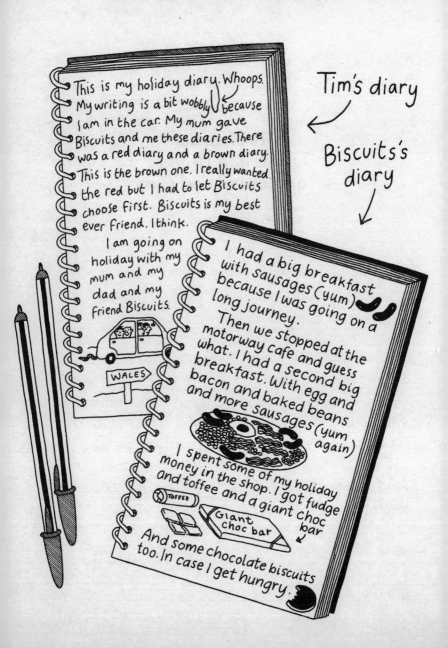

This is my holiday diary. Whoops. My writing is a bit wobbly because I am in the car. My mum gave Biscuits and me these diaries. There was a red diary and a brown diary. This is the brown one. I really wanted the red but I had to let Biscuits choose first. Biscuits is my best ever friend. I think.

I am going on holiday with my mum and my dad and my friend Biscuits.

WALES

Tim's diary

Biscuits's diary

I had a big breakfast with sausages (yum) because I was going on a long journey.

Then we stopped at the motorway cafe and guess what. I had a second big breakfast. With egg and bacon and baked beans and more sausages (yum again)

I spent some of my holiday money in the shop. I got fudge and toffee and a giant choc bar

TOFFEE

Giant choc bar

And some chocolate biscuits too. In case I get hungry.

I'd been looking forward to my holiday for ages and ages. We were going to this seaside place in Wales called Llanpistyll. It is a funny name. It's spelled funny too. It's in Wales and lots of Welsh words are peculiar. Dad says it's a super place though. He went there when he was a boy.

'We had such fun, me and my brothers,' said Dad. 'We swam every day and we made a camp and we played French cricket on the beach and we went for long clifftop walks.'

'I don't want to go on any clifftop walks,' said Mum. 'I hate it when people go too near the edge.'

'*I* won't go too near the edge, Mum,' I said.

I hate heights too. I went abseiling once. I *had* to. It was an adventure holiday. It was s-o-o-o-o scary.

'Shame you haven't got any brothers, Tim,' said Dad. 'It won't be such fun for you.'

'We can have fun together,' said Mum. 'What are the shops like at Llanpistyll?'

'Shops?' said Dad. 'I *think* there's one.'

'*One?*' said Mum. 'What sort of shop?'

'I don't know. A general store, I suppose,' said Dad impatiently. 'You don't go to Llanpistyll to go *shopping*.'

'Obviously not,' said Mum. She sighed. 'I like shopping.'

'So do I,' I said.

Dad sighed too. Even more impatiently.

'Boys don't like shopping,' he said. 'I worry about you sometimes, Tim.'

I worry about my dad sometimes too. He doesn't half go on. And on and on.

'We have a lovely time when we go shopping at the Flowerfields centre on Saturdays, don't we, Tim?' said Mum.

'Tim should be having fun with his friends, not hanging round his mum,' said Dad. Then he stopped and snapped his fingers. 'I've had a brilliant idea!'

I twitched. I don't always like my dad's ideas. Particularly when he thinks they're brilliant. But this time *I* thought it a Truly Dazzling idea.

'Let's invite one of Tim's friends to come

to Llanpistyll too,' said Dad.

'Oh *yes*!!!' I said.

'Oh no!' said Mum. 'I'm not at all sure about looking after someone else's child. And some of those boys in Tim's class at school are a pretty wild bunch.'

'I don't want to invite anyone from school,' I said. 'I want to invite Biscuits!'

'That boy you met on the adventure holiday?' said Mum.

'The boy who was always eating?' said Dad.

'He seemed quite a nice well-behaved sort of boy,' said Mum. 'Better than that Kelly!'

I met this girl Kelly on the adventure holiday too. She's my girlfriend now. I didn't really choose her. She chose me. She keeps writing to me. She puts all these kisses at the end. It's dead embarrassing. But she's OK really. Quite good fun actually. But nowhere *near* as much fun as Biscuits.

So Dad got in touch with Biscuits's dad. And Mum had a long talk on the phone with Biscuits's mum. It was all fixed!

I was thrilled. Biscuits was thrilled.

Kelly was not at all thrilled when I wrote and told her.

She wrote back: 'You mean rotten stinking pig. Why didn't you ask *me* to go to this

103

Llanpissy place with you??? Though I'm going to have a MUCH better holiday. My mum's got this new boyfriend with a caravan and we're all going to go camping and it'll be heaps more fun. And I *might* have asked you to come too but I'm not now. So there.'

I got a bit worried I might have upset Kelly.

'But Kelly's just my *girl*friend. Biscuits is my best ever *friend* friend,' I said to Mum. 'I'm so so so pleased he's coming on holiday. We'll have such fun together. We laughed and mucked around and played all these daft games together when we were on that adventure holiday. It was great.'

'I thought you said you'd had a terrible time,' said Mum. 'Oh dear. I think I'd better buy a good book for this holiday.'

She sounded a bit huffy. I got the feeling I'd somehow upset her too.

'It's only natural that Tim wants to play games with his pal. Do you know how to play French cricket, Tim? It's a great game – but you'll need me to join in too, to make up the numbers.'

'Biscuits and me don't like French or cricket, Dad. We play our own games. He's Biscuits-Boy and I'm Super-Tim,' I said.

'Oh. Right. I see,' said Dad. He suddenly sounded huffy too.

I seemed to have upset everyone.

I felt upset myself the morning of the holiday. Truly seriously upset. I felt sick and shaky and my tummy kept squeezing so I couldn't eat my breakfast.

'Oh dear, oh dear, I do hope you're not going down with anything nasty, Tim,' said Mum, feeling my forehead.

'He's fine. He's just tired because it's so early,' said Dad, yawning.

It was *ever* so early, still practically night time. We had to make an early start because Llanpistyll is a very long way.

'We've had to make an even earlier start than usual to pick up Biscuits on the way. You do realize, Tim, it's adding a good fifty miles to the journey,' said Dad.

'Biscuits is such a silly name. I hope he's not a silly boy. I don't want you two messing around too much, Tim. I don't like it when you get over-excited,' said Mum. 'Is that why you're feeling funny, dear? Because you're so looking forward to seeing him?'

I didn't know. I suddenly felt *shy*. I knew I liked Biscuits ever so much. But what if he didn't like me this time? Maybe he'd changed? Maybe he'd think me a bit weird now? And what would he think of my mum and dad?

I'd packed Walter Bear in my suitcase but I had to rush to my bedroom and get him out and have a quick nuzzle into his warm furry head. Then I saw myself in the mirror.

I saw this boy and this bear having a cuddle. Maybe Biscuits would think me a great big *baby*?

'Come *on*, Tim, I thought you'd done all your packing,' said Dad, peering round my door. 'Put that silly bear down and get a move on.'

Dad certainly thought me a great big baby. I don't think he likes Walter Bear one bit.

'Do you *really* have to take that old bear with you?' said Dad.

'Yes, I really have to, Dad,' I said clinging to Walter.

'Well, pack it away, then! You don't want Biscuits to laugh at you, do you?' said Dad, and he snatched Walter and shoved him on top of my folded holiday clothes and slammed the case shut.

'Dad! Watch out! His legs are all twisted back – and his nose will get squashed! He wants me to make him a special nest in my T-shirts,' I wailed.

'Oh give me strength!' said Dad. 'You mind I don't pack *you* in the suitcase too. Now go and get in the car this minute while I lock up the house and get the boot loaded.'

'No, wait! Tim, have you done a last wee?' said Mum.

'Yes!'

'When? I should do another one just in case,' said Mum.

I wondered if Mum would keep asking if I needed to have a wee when Biscuits was around. Maybe Dad was right. Maybe he *would* laugh at me.

It was a very long drive up to where Biscuits lived. I sat. I looked out the window. I bit my nails.

'Are you all right, Tim? You're ever so quiet,' said Mum. 'You're not feeling sick, are you?'

'A bit,' I said.

'Oh, dear,' said Mum. 'Here, have a barley sugar. Maybe we should have given you a travel pill. Wind the window down a bit, dear. If you really feel you're going to be sick, do try to tell Dad in time, won't you?'

'He's not going to be sick,' said Dad. 'Don't keep on about it. Try to take his mind off it.'

'Well, I've got some little treats in my bag – but I was going to wait until Biscuits could share them too. Why don't you just cuddle up with Walter Bear, Tim?'

'I *can't*. He's shut in the suitcase. With his legs bent back and his nose squashed sideways,' I said mournfully.

'Do give it a rest – both of you!' said Dad.

Mum went into a huff.

I went in a huff too, though I'm not sure Dad noticed.

Then I fell asleep for a bit.

'Wake up, Tim!' Dad called. 'We're nearly at Biscuits's house. Now, according to this map they sent, Marlow Road should be . . . oh blow, we've just gone past it!'

It took another ten minutes of turning down one-way roads and doing U-turns before we eventually arrived outside Biscuits's house. And there was Biscuits on the doorstep.

'There he is! Well, get out the car, Tim, and run and say hello,' said Dad.

'We'll all get out, darling,' said Mum. 'Come on. What's the matter? You're not shy, are you?'

I felt s-o-o-o-o shy I couldn't say a word.

Biscuits didn't seem the slightest bit shy.

'Hey, Tim! I've been looking out for you for ages! Hi, Mrs Parsons, Mr Parsons. My mum says do you want to come inside for a cup of tea?'

'It's very kind of you but we'd better get on our way,' said Dad.

All the same, the two mums talked for ten minutes about mealtimes and bedtimes and boring stuff like that, and the two dads talked about motorways and petrol and boring stuff like *that*.

'We could have had a cup of tea after all,' said Biscuits. '*And* biscuits.'

'Are you hungry, dear? said Mum.

'You bet,' said Biscuits.

'Well, we'll stop at a motorway café quite soon,' said Mum.

'Great,' said Biscuits. He nudged me. 'Great, Tim, yeah?'

'Yeah,' I said. My voice was still all little and whispery.

'Tim's feeling a bit shy,' Mum announced.

I could have kicked her. Everyone looked at me. I went red.

'Do you think you ought to have a quick wee while we're here, Tim?' Mum said. She lowered her voice a bit this time – but everyone still heard. I went redder than ever.

I wouldn't go, even though I quite wanted to. Biscuits said goodbye to his mum and dad and then we got in the car and set off.

'Would you boys like a barley sugar?' said Mum, passing us the bag.

'Yes please,' said Biscuits. He put three in

his mouth at once and sucked happily. 'Yum, I'm starving.'

'We'll stop at the first café we come to when we're on the motorway,' Mum said.

Dad wanted to carry on driving but Mum said Biscuits could obviously do with a proper breakfast. So we stopped at the first service station. We made a trip to the toilets first. I had to dash to get there in time. Then we went to the cafeteria. Mum and I just had tea and toast. Dad said he might as well have a fry-up now he was here.

'That sounds a great idea,' said Biscuits. 'Can I have one too? With bacon and lots of sausages? Yum!'

'You've certainly got a healthy appetite, young man,' said Dad.

'I think it's an *un*healthy appetite,' said a funny squeaky voice. Something pink and knitted popped out of Biscuits's pocket.

'It's Dog Hog!' I said. 'I'd forgotten all about him! It's your doggy piggy thing your granny knitted.'

'Yes, I'm Dog Hog. Fancy forgetting me!' Biscuits made Dog Hog say. He pretended to poke me with one of his floppety arms. Then Dog Hog gave Biscuits a poke too. 'You're not to eat bacon or sausages! They might very well be my distant relations.'

'Well, your distant relations taste ever so yummy,' said Biscuits cheerily.

'Horrid greedy boy,' said Dog Hog. Biscuits made Dog Hog's head wobble from side to side.

'What's he looking for?' I said.

'I'm looking for a certain Mr Bear I've heard a lot about,' said Dog Hog.

'Oh, you want to meet Walter Bear!' I said. 'Well, he's all stuffed into my suitcase at the moment, isn't he, Dad?'

Dad sighed – but his big breakfast had put him in a good mood. When we got back in the car he got my suitcase out of the boot and pulled Walter Bear out.

Poor poor Walter Bear. I straightened his legs very gently. He lay back stiffly in my arms, his entire snout squashed out of shape.

'I don't think he's been able to breathe a bit!' I said, trying to rub his nose back into position.

'Here, let Dog Hog get at him,' said Biscuits, and he made Dog Hog bend over and put his woolly mouth on Walter's.

'What *is* he doing? *Kissing* him?' I said.

'No! He's giving him artificial respiration,' said Biscuits.

'Oh, right,' I said happily. I pummelled Walter Bear's furry chest. 'I'll help too. Come on, Walter, start breathing again.'

I made Walter take a great big breath and sit up.

'Ah! Thank you so much,' I made him say, in a deep growly voice. 'Who is this kind pink person, Tim? He's certainly saved my bacon. Whoops! Pardon the expression.'

'This is Dog Hog, Walter Bear.'

'I like Dog Hog, Tim,' said Walter Bear.

'So do I,' I said.

And I liked Biscuits too. Ever so much. I wasn't shy any more. Not one bit.

'I'm glad you're coming on holiday with us, Biscuits,' I said.

'Me too!' said Biscuits. 'Hey, I'm glad this isn't an adventure holiday like last time.'

'You can say that again!'

'I'm glad this isn't an adventure holiday like last time.'

'You can say that again!'

We both started cracking up laughing.

But we were *wrong*.

This holiday was going to be Truly Terribly Adventurous!

Chapter Two
Tim's diary

I am here and guess what. Dad is right. LLanpistyll is brilliant. Biscuits and I get the giggles whenever we say LLanpistyll. We say it a lot. HEAPS of things have happened. Biscuits nearly committed a murder.

Eek!

And I built the Eighth Wonder of the World (miniature version) but then it was destroyed by a Deadly Fiendish Enemy.

D.F.E.'s mate

Biscuits's diary

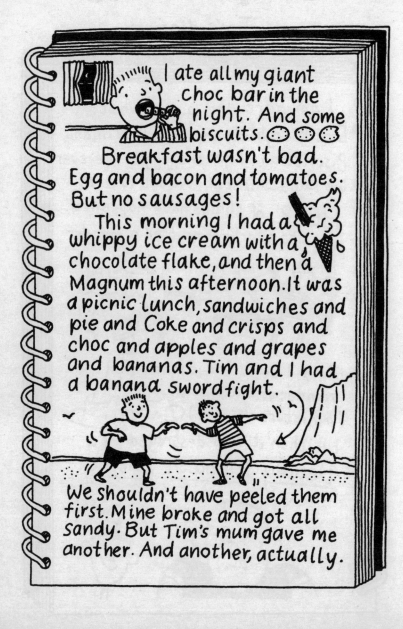

I ate all my giant choc bar in the night. And some biscuits.

Breakfast wasn't bad. Egg and bacon and tomatoes. But no sausages!

This morning I had a whippy ice cream with a chocolate flake, and then a Magnum this afternoon. It was a picnic lunch, sandwiches and pie and Coke and crisps and choc and apples and grapes and bananas. Tim and I had a banana swordfight.

We shouldn't have peeled them first. Mine broke and got all sandy. But Tim's mum gave me another. And another, actually.

Our hotel was called the Gwesty Bryn Nodfa. Gwesty is Welsh for hotel. We were guests in the Gwesty. There weren't many other guests because it's quite a little hotel.

Two old ladies looked out of the Gwesty guest lounge and saw Biscuits and me and said, 'Oh dear! *Boys!* They'll start rampaging around in their great big boots.'

So Biscuits whispered in my ear, 'Oh dear! *Old ladies!* They'll start rampaging around in their great big Scholl sandals.'

I cracked up laughing. Biscuits did too.

Mum frowned at us.

'Boys! Calm down now.' She looked apologetically at the old ladies. 'Don't worry, they're very well-behaved boys.'

'But I bet they're very badly behaved old

115

ladies,' Biscuits whispered.

I cracked up laughing again. Biscuits did too. We couldn't stop even when Mum got really cross. Biscuits laughed so much he choked on the last bit of a Kit Kat he'd been munching and he had to be patted on the back. Little bits of Kit Kat – Kitten Krumbs – spattered out of his mouth and slurped down his chin.

'Really!' said Mum, whipping out her hankie.

'Oh leave the boys be. It's just high spirits,' said Dad. 'Come on, don't let's bother with unpacking. Let's get on the beach while the sun's still out.'

So we walked to the beach. We loped down all these little lanes with hedges full of honeysuckle and wild roses and harebells. We spotted one hedgehog and two butterflies and three rabbits and four magpies. Mum said it seemed a very long way to this beach.

Then we had to skirt round a cabbage field and Biscuits and I had a long discussion about the general disgustingness of cabbage. Even Biscuits isn't keen on eating something that pongs of old drains. Mum said she was sure we were lost and she was getting a blister.

Then we had to climb over a stile. It was

fun sorting out which way to put your legs. Dad said they were also called kissing gates. He helped Mum climb over and when she was balancing at the top he kissed her! I was dead embarrassed. Biscuits and I raised our eyebrows and made smarmy sucky kissing noises. Mum went very pink but she didn't tell us off. Her blister didn't seem to be hurting her any more because she didn't lag behind. She bounced along arm in arm with Dad, while Biscuits and I ran ahead because we could see the sea at last.

'Careful!' Mum shouted. 'Don't go too near the edge, boys!'

But we weren't at the top of a steep chalky cliff. It was all sandy grass and then there was just a long slope of wonderful soft sand in front of us, down down down to the beach.

'Wheeeeeeee!' shouted Biscuits, and he started sliding down on his bottom.

'Wheeeeeeee!' I shouted too, sliding likewise.

I had sand all up my T-shirt and shorts but I didn't care a bit. I leaned over sideways and tumbled over and over, shrieking.

'Wow!' said Biscuits, and he turned sideways and started tumbling too.

He looked like a great big beachball bouncing all the way down.

By the time I got to the bottom I had sand

in my hair and my ears and my mouth and even up my nose but I still didn't care. I just took off my T-shirt and rubbed it all off. Biscuits did the same.

'Keep your T-shirts *on*, boys. You don't want to get sunburnt!' Mum called.

She rubbed us all over with this sunscreen stuff. It was ever so tickly and Biscuits and I both got the giggles. Then the sun went in and soon we needed our T-shirts back on, *and* our sweaters.

'How about a game of French cricket to get warm?' said Dad.

'Oh Dad. No! I hate games like that,' I said.

'You've never even played it. Come on, it's *fun*, Tim,' said Dad.

'Why don't you all make a nice sandcastle?' said Mum quickly.

'Oh yes!' I said.

I know about castles. I did this special project at school.

'Let's build a motte and bailey castle, eh, Biscuits?' I said.

'You what?' said Biscuits. 'Bot and naily?'

'You twit! Motte. That's a castle that's up on a mound, right? And the bailey is the walk right round it.'

'No, don't let's build a boring old motte and bailey castle, Tim. We'll do my bot and naily

118

castle. All the soldiers stand up the top and moon at the enemy showing their bots, right?'

'OK, OK,' I said, giggling. 'And then they cut off all their horny old toenails and flick them over the parapets so that it's like confetti and all these daggy old nailies get in the enemies' hair, right, Biscuits?'

'What on earth are you two going on about?' said Dad, getting a bit irritated. 'OK, let's build a sandcastle.'

There was just one problem. We didn't have any decent spades. There was a little kiosk right along at the top of the beach so we trailed all the way there but they just had little baby plastic spades for toddlers. They had ice-cream though so we had that instead.

I was a bit disappointed. I had this vision of a brilliant turreted castle on a mound with *garderobes* and arrow-slit windows and a little drawbridge. But Biscuits licked his ice-cream happily and didn't seem to mind a bit.

When we went back to the hotel I spotted something in the umbrella stand in the hall. Two big spades with painted wooden handles and hard metal blades. They were very old and chipped but still sturdy. They looked as if they'd been lolling in the umbrella stand a very long time.

The hotel lady, Mrs Jones, made a fuss of

119

Biscuits at dinner because he had mushroom soup and a roll and then chicken and chips and peas and then apple pie and cream and he said it was all extra yummy, especially the pie. Mrs Jones said it was her own special home-made pie and she brought him another slice because she said it was good to see a young man who appreciated his food.

I hadn't been able to finish my pie and I didn't like the skin on my chicken and I don't like soup, especially not mushroom.

Mum apologized for me being such a picky eater but Mrs Jones just laughed and ruffled my hair. She seemed to like me too even though I don't appreciate my food like Biscuits. So I plucked up courage to ask about the spades.

'Those old spades, dearie? Of course you two boys can borrow them.'

'Wow! Great!' I said.

'Wow and wow again and great and even greater,' said Biscuits.

We went to inspect the spades in the umbrella stand while Mum and Dad had coffee.

'I'll have the one with the red handle,' said Biscuits, grabbing it.

'But you had the red holiday diary,' I said.

120

'Yes, so red's my colour,' said Biscuits. 'You can have the blue.'

'But I was the one who asked about the spades,' I said. 'And I let you have first pick of the holiday diaries so I should have first pick now.'

'It's only an old *spade*,' said Biscuits, but he hung on to it. He lifted it in the air like a sword. 'I challenge you to a duel, Super-Tim.'

'OK, OK, Biscuits-Boy,' I said, seizing the blue spade reluctantly.

I hoped he was joking. Biscuits seemed a lot stronger than me – and the spades were heavy, with sharp edges.

Biscuits lunged. I dodged. Biscuits went on lunging, slightly off balance – and very nearly speared one of the old ladies shuffling out of the dining room. She shrieked. Her friend shrieked too. Mum came running and she shrieked as well. She couldn't get cross with Biscuits because he was our guest. So she got cross with me. Which wasn't fair. Not one bit.

'Sorry you got the telling off, Tim,' Biscuits said, when we were in our room.

'It's OK,' I said, though I was still feeling ever so miffed.

'Look. You can have the red spade if you really want it,' said Biscuits.

'It's OK,' I repeated, not quite so miffed.

'I insist,' said Biscuits.

'Right! The red spade's mine,' I said, suddenly not miffed at all. I giggled. 'You didn't half make that old lady jump, Biscuits.'

'I nearly skewered her like a kebab,' said Biscuits, and he giggled too.

We mimed the mock duel all over again. We couldn't act it out because we'd been told *very firmly* that the spades had to be kept in the umbrella stand all the time we were in the hotel.

We had a duel with our toothbrushes instead and that was great fun, even though Biscuits kept winning. Then Mum came in to settle us down and she made a bit of a fuss about the frothy toothpaste all over everywhere but she didn't get too narky this time.

'I suppose boys will be boys,' she said. 'Now, it's been a long day and you were up very early, Tim. Time to snuggle down and go to sleep.'

We snuggled down. But of course we didn't go to sleep. We held an amazingly rude competition. Then we had a joke-telling bonanza. Biscuits knows some wonderfully disgusting jokes. I snorted so much I had to bury my head in the pillow. So did Biscuits. And then he realized he'd lain on his night-time emergency pack of biscuits. There were an awful lot of crumbs. He had to eat them all up to get rid of them.

Then he nodded off. Biscuits makes little munching noises even in his sleep. Then I went to sleep too and dreamed I was down on the beach, building the biggest sandcastle in the world. I stepped inside and explored, climbing the narrow steps round and round, right to the top of the golden tower . . .

Then I woke up and it was morning. The first thing I thought of was Castle.

Then Biscuits woke up and the first thing he did was sniff hopefully.

'Hi, Biscuits! Are you seeing if you can smell the sea air?'

'Hi, Tim! No, I'm seeing if I can sniff sausages for breakfast!' said Biscuits.

'No, no, no, Mr Cannibal,' said Dog Hog, struggling out from under the sheets and attacking Biscuits.

Walter Bear and I watched, cuddling peacefully.

'You are crackers, Biscuits,' I said. 'Hey, can I really have the red spade today?'

'Well, I said you could have it yesterday so really it should be my turn today,' said Biscuits.

'But I never got to use it yesterday!' I said indignantly.

'I'll fight you for the spade, right?' said Biscuits, and he picked up his pillow and thumped me with it.

I thumped back with mine.

We were soon bouncing backwards and forwards on the beds, thumping and bumping, clouting and shouting. Shouting a little too loudly.

'Boys, boys! Stop it at once!' Mum hissed, rushing into our room in her nightie and dressing gown. 'Honestly! What am I going to do with you? It isn't seven o'clock yet and you're already behaving like horrible hooligans. Now get back into bed and try to have another little snooze.'

We didn't feel the least bit sleepy. We had another weeny-teeny pillow fight, and Biscuits called me a horrible hooligan and I called Biscuits a horrible hooligan. Then we did a horrible hooligan dance, swaying our hips to be hula-hula hooligans, and Biscuits swayed so much his pyjamas fell down round his ankles. I laughed so hard I fell over in a heap on my bed. Mum came in, Mega-Mad, saying we were waking up all the other guests in the Gwesty and there would be Complaints at Breakfast.

But no-one did complain, though the old lady Biscuits had practically skewered flinched

124

nervously as he thundered past her table. Mum was still a bit narky but Dad cheered her up by suggesting we drive to the nearest small town and buy some picnic food and maybe have a little look round the shops.

'Oh n-o-o-o-o-o-o. Biscuits and I want to go straight on the beach with our spades,' I wailed.

But Biscuits seemed to think picnic food might be a seriously good idea, so I didn't make too much fuss. We went to a town called Abercoch. Another name that gave Biscuits and me the giggles. Dad went on about how big it had become and moaned like anything about the amusement arcades and caravan sites and the supermarket in the town centre.

Mum went on about how small it was and why didn't it have a Marks & Spencer and weren't there any decent clothes shops at all? But after we'd got the food we all had an ice-cream and then we got back in the car and parked it at the Gwesty Bryn Nodfa and collected all our beach stuff (including the spades) and walked along the footpaths and around the fields and over the stile and ran all the way down the sandy slope and AT LAST we were on the beach.

I was all set to build the best castle in the world. But guess what. The tide was in. Right in, so that the water was way up, lapping the skirts of the sandy slope. There was barely room to put down our towels and picnic.

'Oh *rats rats rats*,' I said. 'I want to build my castle!'

'Don't say "rats" like that, dear. Now, never mind. You can sit down quietly with Biscuits and read your comics or do some writing in your holiday diaries,' said Mum.

'Never mind, Tim, we can all go for a swim,' said Dad.

'Never mind, Tim, we can maybe have our picnic now instead,' said Biscuits.

'But I wanted to build my *castle*.'

I tried digging in the soft powdery sand of the slope but it was useless. It just slithered and slopped around and wouldn't stand firm at all.

'It's not *fair*.'

'Oh Tim, don't be such a baby,' said Dad. 'Stop making such a fuss about a silly sand-castle. Let's go for a swim.'

'Are you sure the sea is clean enough? You hear such horrible tales about pollution nowadays,' said Mum.

'It's clear as crystal. You come in too,' said Dad.

'Somebody's got to sit here and mind all the picnic things,' said Mum.

'I'll do that,' said Biscuits.

He wasn't all that keen on swimming either. But Dad practically pulled us in.

It was f-r-e-e-z-i-n-g. Biscuits and I stood shivering, hugging our elbows, knees knocking, feet solid ice.

'Come on, you two, get in properly,' Dad yelled. 'It's lovely once you're under.' His teeth were chattering too, and his face was purple.

'This isn't my idea of fun,' said Biscuits.

'You can say that again,' I said.

'This isn't my idea of fun,' said Biscuits.

'You can say that— aaaah!' I yelled, because Dad suddenly splashed me.

I splashed him back. And Biscuits. They both splashed each other. And me. Suddenly we were all jumping about and it wasn't quite so cold. It was almost fun.

It was freezing again afterwards, on the beach getting dry, but then we had our picnic and this was very *much* Biscuits' idea of fun – and mine too.

Afterwards Mum laid back and had a little sunbathe. Dad did too. They both started snoring gently, little smiles under their sunhats.

'Let's build our castle!' I said joyfully, because the tide had gone out far enough now and had left gleaming wet wondrous sand just waiting for us to build the best sandcastle in the world.

So we set to, Biscuits and me. I pretty soon realized it wasn't going to be as easy-peasy as I'd thought, even with good sand and sharp spades.

'It's a bit too much like hard work,' Biscuits panted, leaning on his spade. 'Shall we have a sunbathe too, Tim?'

'No, let's make the castle, *please*. Look, you gather shells and seaweed and stuff for decoration if you want a bit of a rest. I'll carry on,' I said nobly.

I carried on. And on and on. I thought of my vision of a castle bigger than me. Now I wondered about a medium-size castle. Or even a small one. I'd only managed a very small mound, so I decided to go for miniature perfection instead of massive bulk.

I squatted down beside my castle and tried to mould it into shape. It was far more finicky than I'd thought. Sand got right up my nails and invaded the legs of my shorts. Little gritty bits embedded themselves in my knees. I tried to fashion a little drawbridge but it was hopeless. My arrow-slit windows weren't exact enough. The tower kept wobbling and collapsing.

'That'll do,' said Biscuits. 'Here, we'll stick

little shells in front to make a path, right?'

'You don't have a *path*. We could make a moat. And fill it with water from the sea.'

'Oh-oh,' said Biscuits. 'Something tells me that sounds like hard work.'

We didn't have a bucket so we had to make do with old paper cups. We ran to the sea and filled them up and ran back to the castle and tipped the water in the proposed moat. It immediately disappeared down through the sand.

'Rats,' I said again. I stared at my lop-sided little castle with its empty moat and sighed. 'It's not much of a castle, is it, Biscuits?'

'I think it's a super castle,' said Biscuits. 'Truly. A fantastic creation. Practically the Eighth Wonder of the World. Honest, Tim.'

'Ooooh! Let's see this super-duper castle, eh?' said a loud voice behind us, making us both jump.

Two boys had crept up behind us. One was about our age and very pale and pinched looking. He didn't look very tough but his smile was spiteful. He was the sort of boy you treated with caution.

The other boy was much bigger. And much tougher too. His hair was shaved so short it was just prickles, which looked as sharp as spikes. If he head-butted you you'd get severely perforated. He was the sort of boy that made Red Alert Alarm system, buzz inside your brain.

He was wearing great big Doc Martens even on the beach. I looked at the boy. I looked at the boots. I knew what was going to happen next.

'What a dinky ducky castle you two little cissy boys have made,' he said, his eyes beady. 'Shame it's just sand. Someone could accidentally trip and . . .'

He kicked hard. The castle collapsed. He laughed. His mate laughed.

'You! You big bully! I saw that! You kicked my Tim's castle over deliberately!'

Oh no. It was Mum. She came rushing towards us, red in the face, her dress still tucked up to get her legs sunburnt.

The boys spluttered with laughter.

'Mummy's boys!' said the big prickly kicker. 'Don't worry. We'll be back.'

They ran off, laughing and laughing.

Biscuits and I didn't laugh at all.

Prickle-Head and Pinch-Face were going to get us!

Chapter Three

Tim's diary

I seem to be in the middle of a Dire and Dangerous Adventure.

The Deadly Fiendish Enemy has made another Evil Advance.

Biscuits-Boy and I are desperately outnumbered. (Well, I know it's two against two. But they're much bigger. Especially Prickle-Head).

However! We have a new recruit to our ranks.

You will never guess who it is.

Biscuits's diary

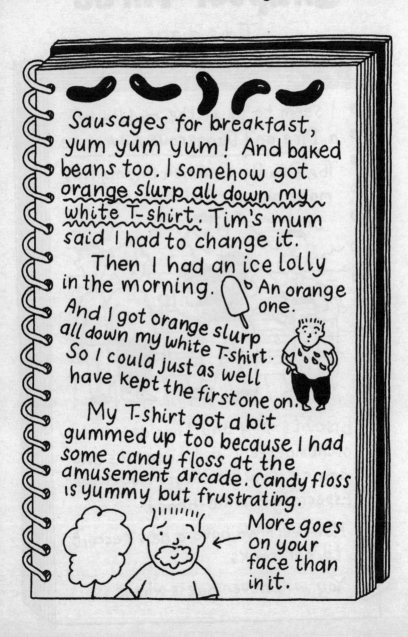

Sausages for breakfast, yum yum yum! And baked beans too. I somehow got orange slurp all down my white T-shirt. Tim's mum said I had to change it.

Then I had an ice lolly in the morning. An orange one.

And I got orange slurp all down my white T-shirt. So I could just as well have kept the first one on.

My T-shirt got a bit gummed up too because I had some candy floss at the amusement arcade. Candy floss is yummy but frustrating.

← More goes on your face than in it.

It was raining when we woke up the next morning.

'Sorry, boys,' said Dad at breakfast. 'It doesn't look like a good day for the beach.'

'Rats!' I said.

'Don't use that silly expression, Tim,' said Mum

'OK. Large twitchy-nosed long-tailed sewer-scavenging rodents!'

'Now, now. No need to be cheeky,' said Mum.

'The boy's just upset because he was dying to get on the beach,' said Dad.

I wasn't *that* upset, actually. Maybe it wouldn't be a bad idea to keep right away from the beach for a bit. Just in case the big prickly boy turned up again with his pinch-faced pal.

Biscuits didn't look as if he minded too much either. He was cheerfully chomping up his third sausage.

'We'll go for a little drive, eh?' said Dad.

'Yes, let's see if we can find a proper shopping centre,' said Mum.

'I was thinking of a scenic country tour,' said Dad.

Mum sighed. So we toured the country. And it was very scenic. And very wet. We saw grey sky and grey mountains and grey sea.

Biscuits and I got fed up being in the car. But then we saw some people walking in the wet, mud all up their legs. They were huddled under their anorak hoods, water dripping down their noses. Maybe it wasn't so bad in the car after all.

We played I Spy. Dad chose C for car and Mum guessed it.

Mum chose C for Church and Biscuits guessed it.

Biscuits chose C for Café and I guessed it.

So I wanted to chose a C too, but I couldn't think of one. Then I saw something way in the distance, at the top of a mound. Something I'd studied, though I'd never seen one in real life before. Something that had been standing, grey in the gloom but golden in the sunlight, for hundreds and hundreds of years.

'I've got one! I spy with my little eye, something beginning with C!'

Dad guessed Clock (inside the car) and Mum guessed Cardigan (on her) and Biscuits guessed Cabbages (in a pongy old field) and I told them to hurry up a bit or we'd be way past it, but Dad turned off right and it was still in sight. We were actually going *towards* my C. When Mum and Dad kept guessing silly things they couldn't possibly see like camels and computers and candlesticks I knew that *they* knew and we were going to look round my special C.

Biscuits still didn't get it.

'Cake?' he said hopefully.

'What about C for Chocolate?' said Mum, reaching into her handbag and bringing out a big bar of Cadbury's Dairy Milk. 'Biscuits?'

'Wow, thank you!' said Biscuits, thinking he was getting the whole bar to himself.

'No, dear! Just take a couple of pieces and then pass the bar to Tim. You couldn't possibly eat a whole big bar yourself,' said Mum.

'I could,' said Biscuits. 'Bigger bars than this. Easy peasy.'

'Biscuits's eating powers are phe-nom-en-al,' I said. 'Hey Biscuits, guess my C, go on.'

'Cadbury's!' said Biscuits.

'Your eating powers might be phenomenal,

but you're totally *useless* at I Spy,' I said, elbowing him in his big soft side.

'Hey, your skinny little elbows aren't half sharp,' said Biscuits, elbowing me back.

'Hey, your great galumping elbows aren't half hard,' I said, shoving him.

He shoved back and we started a Mega-Wrestle in the back of the car.

'Boys! Boys! Stop fighting!' Mum shouted.

'They're only messing about,' said Dad.

'They'll choke on their chocolate,' said Mum.

'Anyway, we're here now,' said Dad, pulling up.

'Here! At my special C word!' I said.

'Could it possibly be a Crumbling Creaky *Castle*?' Biscuits laughed, and had another big bite of the chocolate bar when Mum wasn't watching.

He winked at me and I winked at him. Then he winked the other eye and I winked my other eye. Then he winked both rapidly so I did too.

'Tim? Have you got something in your eye, dear? Come here and let me have a look,' said Mum.

'It's nothing, Mum. Don't keep *fussing*,' I said, getting out the car.

'This awful rain,' said Mum. 'You'd better

both come under my umbrella, boys.'

'Oh Mum, it's only little drops of water,' I said impatiently. 'Come on, Biscuits-Boy, race you to the top of the tower!'

'Now slow down, Tim. You're not to rush off up anywhere. Old castles can be very danger- ous,' said Mum. 'Especially when it's all slippery in the wet. *Tim!*'

'Don't worry, *I'm* not rushing,' said Biscuits.

It took him *ages* and *ages* to get right to the top of the tower. He had to have lots of rests. So did Mum. And even Dad got a bit puffed.

I got to the top FIRST. I've never ever won a proper race before. I'm hopeless going along the ground. I nearly always come last. But I can fly upwards like a rocket. I spread my arms when I was all alone at the top. I stared straight up at the sky, rain pattering on my hot face. I pretended I was really Super-Tim and I'd just whizzed my way over the moun- tains quick as a wink and now I was waiting to meet up with my trusty companion Biscuits- Boy. Waiting and waiting and waiting.

Biscuits had to sit down when he got to the top. His face was purple.

'Are you all right, Biscuits?' I asked.

He couldn't catch his breath to speak. He shook his head instead.

'Why don't you have a biscuit to make you feel better?' I suggested.

'Don't be silly, Tim, the poor boy might choke,' said Mum.

'A – little – piece – of – choco – late – might – help,' Biscuits wheezed.

'I really don't think you ought to eat quite so much chocolate, dear,' said Mum. 'It's really not very good for you. Hasn't your mother tried to put you on a diet?'

Biscuits's eyes popped in horror.

'My – mum – says – I – need – to – eat – lots – to – keep – my – strength – up!' he gasped.

'Yes, dear, but it's being so heavy that makes you so out of breath,' said Mum.

'Now, now, leave the lad alone. It's not really any of our business,' said Dad. 'Come and look at this fantastic view.'

'I don't want to go too near the edge, it makes me feel so dizzy,' said Mum. 'Don't you go near the edge either, boys.'

I didn't want to go right to the edge of the parapet. I didn't mind at all looking *up* but I knew exactly what it would feel like looking *down*. I went a bit wobbly just thinking about it.

'It's – perfectly – safe,' said Biscuits, his voice stronger now. He pulled a face at my mum's back. I hesitated. Then I pulled one too. We both giggled.

'She doesn't half flap, your mum,' Biscuits whispered.

'Yes, I know. Flap, flap, flap,' I said.

It felt such *fun* to whisper about my mum – but my heart had started to thump.

Biscuits raised his big arms and flapped them. I flapped mine too.

Mum turned round, hanging on to Dad.

'What are you two up to?' she called, looking at our rotating arms.

'We're just pretending to fly, Mum, that's all,' I said quickly.

'Come on, let's peer over,' said Biscuits.

'I don't want to,' I said.

'Look, *I* didn't want to clamber up all those millions and millions of steps so that I practically had a heart attack. But I did. Because you wanted to climb the castle. It's stupid to get right up here and then not even look out. Come on. I want to. So it's only fair that you come too.'

I didn't want to let him down. I knew he was still miffed at my mum. I didn't want him to be miffed at me too. So I took his great plump paw and let him drag me towards the edge of the parapet. It came up to my chin but when I glimpsed the ground far below, the crumbling bricks seemed only ankle height. One small step and I'd be walking into thin air, tumbling down down down to the distant grey slabs below.

I gave a little gasp and shut my eyes tight.

'Wow!' said Biscuits. 'You can see for Mega-Miles, even in the rain. OK, so there's the sea. Which little bay is Llanpistyll? And what about Abercoch? Is it that way – or that?'

'I'm not sure,' I mumbled, pretending to be peering. I had my hands up near my closed eyes so Biscuits wouldn't suss anything.

'And can you see that *other* castle? It's huge! It's got *two* towers! And a proper drawbridge and a real moat!' said Biscuits.

'Where?' I said, opening my eyes. I held on to the edge of the parapet so hard my knuckles nearly sprang straight out of my skin. 'I can't see any castle!'

'Funny! Neither can I, now,' said Biscuits, grinning. 'Must have been a mirage. Still – got you looking, didn't it?'

I stuck my tongue out at him. It wasn't quite so scary now that I was getting used to looking. I liked seeing all the wiggly wavy edges of the coast, just like the maps you do at school. It was weird having an eagle-eye view of the world. I stared at the mustard and cress forests, the saucer-size lake, the pencil spire of the tiny toy church, the little match-box caravan sites until my eyes watered.

I started to enjoy looking across.

I still wasn't so keen on looking directly *down*. But old Biscuits was leaning right *over*.

'Careful, Biscuits!' I said, grabbing him.

'I'm OK. Don't you start flapping now. Here, what's that jutting out bit with the hole? Is that where they poured boiling oil on the invading army?'

I bent my head, my blood pounding. I saw what Biscuits was looking at and laughed wildly.

'No, but it would work almost as well! That's their toilet! They'd do it and it would splash right down so if you were walking about underneath it could land right on your head.'

'*Yuck!*'

We started miming the whole process.

'What on earth are you two boys up to now?' Mum called. 'Why are you rubbing your hair like that, Tim?'

'Oh, I'm just getting a bit wet, that's all,' I said.

'Well, let's go back down and get in the car,' said Mum. 'I wonder if there are any toilets nearby? Tim? Biscuits? What are you two boys laughing at now?'

141

We found the public toilets – modern version – and then got back in the car and did another little scenic tour. Biscuits casually mentioned chocolate once or twice but Mum said it was too near lunchtime.

We drove to Abercoch. It was only drizzling now so we walked along the seafront and had fish and chips out of a packet, all of us sitting on the wet wall. Mum made us put newspaper down first so that we wouldn't get piles. That made us remember this seriously awful sneery-jeery show-off at the adventure holiday place called Giles – only Biscuits called him Piles.

Mum and Dad had take-away cups of tea and we had ice lollies, and then we went for a walk towards the old broken-down pier.

There was a white wooden kiosk near the entrance with all sorts of painted magic symbols round the door and a sign that said GYPSY ROSE, FORTUNE-TELLER TO THE STARS.

'Ooh look,' said Mum. 'I've always wanted to have my fortune told.'

'Don't be so wet,' said Dad. 'It's all a complete con.'

'No, it's not,' said Mum. 'You don't know anything about it. Tim, shall I have my fortune told?'

'Ooh yes, Mum! Can I have my fortune done too?'

'No dear, it's only for grown-ups.'

'You don't want to waste your money,' said Dad.

'Yes I do,' said Mum.

'She'll just tell you some old rubbish about a romantic encounter with a handsome stranger,' said Dad.

'That sounds good to me,' said Mum, knocking at the little wooden door. 'Keep an eye on the boys while I'm in here.'

'Oh, Mum, can't we come and watch?' I said.

But we had to trail after Dad onto the pier. I hung back.

'What's up, Tim?' said Biscuits. 'Look, *I'll* tell your fortune if you like.' He pulled his T-shirt off and tied it round his head like a gypsy scarf. 'Give me your hand, young man. Aah, what's this I see? An encounter with an *ugly* stranger – one with prickly hair and big boots!'

'I hope not!' I said, snatching my hand away – even though I knew he was just larking around.

'Come *on*, you two,' Dad called to us. 'Biscuits, put your T-shirt on, it's hardly sunbathing weather. And what's up with you, Tim?'

'I don't like the pier,' I mumbled.

'What?' said Dad. 'What are you on about? Let's go and see if the lads fishing have caught anything.'

'I don't think much of this pier either,' Biscuits said. 'It's all old and boring. Only one ice-cream stall. They haven't got any dough-nuts or rock or burger bars.'

'Yes, rotten old pier,' I said, though I didn't care about the lack of food stalls.

I didn't like the pier itself. I worried about the way the wooden planks were seldom per-fectly slotted together. You could see through the gaps down to the frothy grey sea under-neath. Some of the planks looked really old, as if they'd splinter as soon as you stepped on them.

I tried to work out the width of the plank and the width of me. It was fine for someone big like Biscuits. But I'm seriously skinny. I could quite possibly go plummeting down-wards to my death. Well, I can swim a bit so maybe I wouldn't drown immediately. But I knew there are all sorts of dangerous currents under piers. Even very strong swimmers could be sucked straight under.

'Why are you walking in that funny way?' asked Biscuits.

'Oh, I – I'm just playing that don't-step-on-the-cracks-game,' I said quickly.

I didn't want to tell Biscuits I was scared of the pier. He'd start to think me the wimpiest wimp ever. He already knew I was scared of heights. And the boy with the prickly hair. (Well, we were *both* a bit scared of him.)

Dad had hurried over to the boys fishing. Biscuits followed. I sidled over, stepping high, holding my breath.

'Maybe we could try a bit of fishing, boys,' Dad said eagerly.

'Yeah, maybe,' said Biscuits. 'Fishing is the sort of sport I like best. You don't rush about. You just sit. And you can eat your fish after!'

I wasn't so sure. I didn't like the idea of being on the pier for ages, especially not perched right at the edge, by the railings.

One of the boys stiffened and hauled in his line.

'He's got one! A real whopper!' said Dad.

We edged nearer to watch. It was a big mistake. A great gasping wriggling pop-eyed fish flapped in the air as it was reeled in. The boy seized it and tore the bait from its mouth, ripping it horribly.

'Oh!' I whispered, covering my own lips.

It got a lot worse. The fish was flopping about frantically, its poor torn mouth an O of agony. The boy held on hard and took aim. I thought he had taken pity on the fish and was going to throw it into the sea. No. He took the gasping fish and whacked its head hard on the wooden planks. The fish stopped flapping. It lay still, a grey slimey sad dead thing.

I felt the fish I'd eaten for lunch flapping inside my tummy. There was a Gents near the end of the pier. I made a run for it, forgetting about the creaking planks in this new emergency. I made it into a cubicle – just. I was very very sick. It was horrible – but it made me feel better too. I didn't want any fish inside me ever again.

Biscuits was waiting for me when I came out.

'Have you been sick?' he asked rather unnecessarily.

'Mmm,' I said, and rinsed my mouth out.

'I'm hardly ever sick,' said Biscuits. 'You must feel horribly empty now. Would you like a biscuit?' He felt in his pocket.

'No thanks!' I said quickly.

'Come and get a bit of fresh air. It's all pongy in here,' said Biscuits.

I must have looked as grey as the poor fish because Biscuits put his arm round me.

'You'll feel better in a minute,' he said, very kindly.

Then we heard a horrible noise from the

very end of the pier. Jeering. And then silly juicy kissy noises.

'Ooh! Look at the little Mummy's boys have a cuddle-wuddle!'

It was Prickle-Head and Pinch-Face, sitting up on the railing at the end of the pier, right beside a sign saying DANGER. The sign was Dead Accurate.

Biscuits sprang away from me as if I was red hot. I certainly felt fiery, blood bubbling in my head like a Jacuzzi.

'Let's go, Biscuits,' I said urgently, starting to back away.

'Biscuits! What sort of a daft poncey name is that?' said Prickle-Head

'It's a nickname, right?' said Biscuits. He added, bravely but unwisely, 'Yours is a lot dafter.'

'So what's *my* nickname, eh?' said Prickle-Head, jumping off the railing and standing in front of Biscuits. Pinch-Face copied him, hands on hips, legs wide apart.

I looked round desperately. Dad was still halfway down the pier, talking to the fishermen.

'Looking for Mumsie-Wumsie to come rushing to the rescue?' said Prickle-Head. 'Ooooh dear. She's not around this time, is she? *Shame!* So, Fatso Big-Bum Biscuits –

what's *my* nickname, eh?'

Biscuits opened his mouth. I knew he was going to come straight out with it. Prickle-Head. Prickle-Head would not be amused. He had his great Doc Martens on. Biscuits was as round as a football. It looked like he was going to get kicked.

'Your nickname's The Boss,' I blurted out.

Biscuits blinked, astonished.

Prickle-Head looked surprised too.

'The Boss?' he repeated slowly, seeking out hidden insulting meanings.

'Yes, we call you The Boss because you're obviously boss of all the beach,' I said.

Prickle-Head sniggered, obviously dead chuffed with his new nickname.

'OK, OK, so I'm The Boss,' he said. 'Check that out, Ricky.'

'Right, Carl,' said Pinch-Face.

'Right, *Boss*,' said Prickle-Head. Then he turned to me. 'What's your nickname then, if your tubby pal is Biscuits? Are you Little Squirt?'

Pinch-Face snorted.

'Yes!' I said. 'Yes, that's me. I'm Little Squirt.'

'Little Squirt and Biscuits,' Prickle-Head repeated.

Pinch-Face snorted so enthusiastically

that a bubble blew out of his nose.

'So, Biscuits,' said Prickle-Head. 'You like them, do you? Biscuits?'

'Yeah, I like them,' said Biscuits.

'Got any biscuits on you, then? How about sharing them round?' said Prickle-Head.

'Sorry. I've eaten my last one,' said Biscuits. Then he added, *so* stupidly, 'and I wouldn't share them with you anyway.'

'You don't want to share your yummy Yoyos and wicked Wagon Wheels and heavenly Hob Nobs?' said Prickle-Head, tutting in a very ominous way. 'Well, we'll see about that. Go through the Fat Boy's pockets, Ricky. They're *bulging* with biscuits.'

'You keep your dirty hands off me,' said Biscuits, clenching his fists.

'Give them your biscuits, Biscuits. We'll get you some more later,' I hissed urgently. 'Don't try to fight them. You won't win.'

I was right. Biscuits hit out but he didn't manage to connect with anything. Prickle-Head kicked out and Biscuits doubled up, Pinch-Face pinioned his arms behind his back and pulled him upright.

I wanted to help him. I really did. But I didn't know *how*.

And I didn't want to get hurt.

Prickle-Head started poking in Biscuits's

pockets. He found biscuits, sweets, chocolate, even a few crushed crisps.

'You greedy pig! You've got a whole corner shop stuffed down your trousers!' Prickle-Head yelled. He gave a last rootle and pulled out something squashed down right at the bottom of Biscuits's pocket. Something woolly.

'What on earth . . . ? Is this your little woolly cardi, Mummy's boy?' said Prickle-Head, shaking the strange pinky-grey object.

It sprouted floppy arms and legs. We were all looking at Dog Hog.

'It's a *cuddly toy*!' Prickle-Head shouted, hardly able to believe his luck.

Pinch-Face shrieked with glee.

Biscuits turned lobster red, as if he were being painfully boiled.

He tried to snatch Dog Hog back but Pinch-Face held him helpless.

I dithered on the edge, desperate. I craned round. Dad was *still* with the fishermen, examining their bait.

'*Dad!*' I yelled. 'Dad come *here*!'

But it was windy on the pier. My voice only carried a few metres. Dad didn't hear me.

'Shut up, Little Squirt,' said Prickle-Head. 'Daddy's not coming and old Mumsie's gone missing. Oh boo-hoo, they want their mummy! Do you need a cuddle with your woolly whatsit, Fat-Bum?'

Prickle-Head dangled Dog Hog in front of Biscuits.

'What *is* it, anyway? It's all long and pink. Hey, is it a woolly willy?'

Pinch-Face squealed.

'Yes, tut, tut, a woolly willy. You don't want to play with a dirty old thing like that,' said Prickle-Head. He suddenly darted to the railings. He leaned over, holding Dog Hog between his finger and thumb.

'Don't!' Biscuits yelled.

'He's only pretending, Biscuits,' I said. '*Dad! Dad!* Look, I'll run for Dad, right?'

'Too late, Little Squirt,' said Prickle-Head, and he dropped Dog Hog over the side.

'Wheeeeee – splosh!' said Prickle-Head, and then he ran off laughing, his big boots thundering on the wooden planks. Pinch-Face ran after him, punching the air.

Biscuits and I rushed to the railings. He'd really dropped Dog Hog but not in the sea. There was a rotting landing stage directly below, and poor Dog Hog lay spread-eagled on it, splashed by the lapping sea.

Biscuits didn't hesitate. He seized the railings and swung his leg over.

'Biscuits! Don't be crazy! You can't! It's

far too dangerous!' I yelled.

'I've got to get Dog Hog. I've had him since I was a baby. My nan knitted him.'

'Then she could knit you another one, Biscuits. Oh please, *don't*!'

'She can't knit another one. She's dead now. I *have* to get him, Tim,' said Biscuits, and he started climbing down determinedly.

'Biscuits! You might fall! *Please* don't. Wait for my dad,' I begged.

'I can't wait,' Biscuits gasped, and then his foot slipped on the wet railing and he was left hanging by his hands.

'*Biscuits!*'

Biscuits held on, got his feet back on the bar below, gave himself a second's breather, and then started feeling for the next bar – and the next – and the next. I hung over the pier, not daring to talk to him any more in case I distracted him. He went down and down – nearly slipped again, hung on – down and down – and then he jumped for it. He was there, on the landing stage!

It creaked ominously as he bounded onto it, as if it might break up altogether under his weight.

'Oh, be careful, Biscuits!' I whispered.

Biscuits seized Dog Hog, held him briefly for one moment, and then stuffed him very firmly far down into his trouser pocket.

'There, I've got him!' said Biscuits. 'Now all I've got to do is get back.'

He looked up. He blinked.

'Ah. The thing is . . . *how* am I going to get back?' Biscuits said.

'I'll *have* to get Dad!' I shouted.

'Are you calling me, Tim?' It *was* Dad, suddenly right beside me. 'What is it? Where's Biscuits?'

'Down there!' I said, pointing.

'*What?*' Dad peered. 'Oh my goodness! Hang on, son. I'll come down.'

'No. I'll come up,' said Biscuits, and he spat on his palms determinedly. He seized the first bar and hauled.

'That's it!' said Dad. 'Now the next!'

Biscuits continued steadily, though his face was purple with effort.

'Steady now,' Dad cried. 'Biscuits? Are you all right? Here, I'm coming!'

'No! I'm – I'm – just – out – of – puff!' Biscuits gasped. 'But – I'm – OK.'

He looked down to see how far he'd got. He wavered.

'Don't look down!' Dad shouted.

Biscuits looked up, and started climbing again.

'That's the lad. Not too far now,' Dad said.

He looked over his shoulder. 'Thank heavens Mum's still with that fortune-teller. She'd go bananas if she saw Biscuits. What's he *playing* at? Don't you boys realize it's highly dangerous?'

'Yes, I realize it ever so, Dad,' I said. 'And so does Biscuits. But this was a serious emergency. You see these boys were being nasty to us and one of them—'

'OK, OK. Don't rabbit on about it now, Tim. Let's just concentrate on Biscuits getting back up here all in one piece,' said Dad, leaning right over and just about reaching Biscuits. 'Take my hand, Biscuits.'

Biscuits did as he was told. Dad very nearly toppled over with his weight, but just about managed to hang on. Biscuits climbed up, and Dad seized him under the armpits and hauled him back over the top of the railings.

Biscuits lay flat on the planks, gasping like the captured fish.

'Are you all right?' Dad asked. He sat down too, and mopped his brow.

'You – bet!' Biscuits puffed.

'Oh Biscuits, you were so *brave!*' I said.

'Yes – I was – wasn't I?' said Biscuits, sitting up and grinning.

'You were also very very reckless and silly,'

said Dad. 'You must never ever do that again, do you promise?'

'Cross my heart and hope to die,' said Biscuits. 'Phew! I feel a bit peckish after all that high drama.'

Prickle-Head had dropped most of Biscuits's secret supply of food. Biscuits started gathering it up and consuming it rapidly.

I didn't feel hungry at all, even though I was ultra-empty after being sick. I still felt bowled over by Biscuits's bravery. And cast down by my own cowardice.

I was a totally useless scaredy-cat little squirt.

I picked my way slowly back down the pier, plank by plank. Biscuits and Dad strode ahead, chatting man to man.

'Are you feeling all right, Tim?' said Mum, but she didn't sound too worried.

The fortune-teller had put her in an unusually good mood.

'She says I'm going to meet someone from the past – and romance is in the air,' said Mum, her eyes sparkling.

'I hope I don't breathe it in – I can't stick romance,' said Biscuits.

Dad laughed and patted him on the back.

They decided they wanted to go to the

amusement arcade. Dad bought us all candy floss. I didn't want mine so I gave it to Biscuits. He started playing this car chase with Dad. Mum began feeding coins into a fruit machine. She didn't listen properly when I started telling her about Prickle-Head and Pinch-Face.

'*What's* his name, darling?' Mum said vaguely – and then she laughed triumphantly. She'd won the jackpot.

'Oh, never mind,' I said huffily, and I wandered off by myself.

I stopped at one of those crane machines full of little rubber trolls with wild pink and purple hair. My girlfriend Kelly has a troll doll called Theresa.

I thought about Kelly. I hoped she wasn't still mad at me for asking Biscuits on holiday instead of her. I decided to try to win her another troll as a holiday present. A friend for Theresa. Yes, she'd really like that. She really liked me. Even if I wasn't very brave.

I put a whole pound coin in the machine. It gave me five goes. It should be easy-peasy to get one troll. Several. Maybe even five.

Ha! I wrestled with the handle that worked the crane but it wouldn't go where I wanted. It missed altogether the first two goes. It caught a troll's hair the third go and I gasped – but the troll slipped away. I missed the fourth time. My hand started to shake for the fifth and final go.

Someone was standing behind me, watching. I *hate* that. The crane opened up its claws. It brushed against a couple of trolls. It knocked one so that its little rubber arm waved cheekily. But then the claws closed on nothing. The crane went up again – empty.

'You're pretty useless!' someone said. 'Here, you'd better let me have a go.'

I turned round to look at this rude stranger.

It wasn't a stranger at all.

It was Kelly!!!

Chapter Four

Tim's diary

Kelly says she is still my girlfriend. She is a lot of fun. But a bit tiring. I think Biscuits is glad Kelly is not his girlfriend.

I am a bit worried because if you have a girlfriend I think you are supposed to protect her from Deadly Enemies. I am useless at this. Kelly says, who cares? She will protect me from Deadly Enemies.

The Enemy is getting deadlier every day.

Maybe we both need to be protected.

Biscuits's diary

We had pizza in Kelly's caravan. We could choose our own toppings. I ordered a pizza with four cheeses and tomato and pepperoni and mushrooms and sweetcorn and artichoke and red pepper and olives and tuna.

Tim's mum said "Are you sure that's everything, Biscuits?" Dead sarcastic.

I said I hadn't ordered broccoli. I don't like green veg. Though actually Kelly's mum left half her artichoke and broccoli pizza and I finished it up for her. I can eat broccoli at a pinch. I can eat anything at a pinch.

Kelly's mum laughed and called me THE HUMAN HOOVER.

I couldn't believe it was Kelly. But there are no other girls like her. She has hair sticking straight up in the air in a top knot. When she's excited it waggles about. She's got little dark glinty eyes and a great big grin. She wears bright clingy clothes and posh trainers and she talks all the time. Well, I suppose there *are* quite a lot of girls like Kelly, but she's the bounciest.

'Kelly!' I said.

'Hi, Tim,' she said. She grinned, the corners of her mouth almost tickling her ears. She had new earrings, white and sparkly. She twiddled them proudly.

'Do you like my diamonds? My mum's boyfriend Dave bought me them as a holiday present,' she said.

'Wow! Real diamonds!' I said.

'Well. Not *real* real. But they're very good synthetic stones,' Kelly said, tossing her head about so that they caught the light. 'Right. Budge over, Tim. I'll show you how to work these cranes.'

Kelly's mum's boyfriend Dave had given her a whole purseful of change. She inserted a coin and started twiddling.

She was *ace*.

In a matter of minutes Theresa Troll had a whole tribe of relations: Tracy Troll and Truman Troll and Tabitha Troll and Tyrone Troll and Tilly Troll and Trocadero Troll. Biscuits and Dad and Mum heard Kelly's triumphant crowing as she kept capturing yet another troll. They came over to watch.

Then Kelly's mum and Kelly's mum's boyfriend Dave and Kelly's little brother Dean and her baby brother Keanu came and watched too. It got very crowded. I'd have died if everyone was watching me. It didn't put Kelly off a bit.

Then all the grown-ups started talking and Kelly's mum's new boyfriend Dave got introduced. He had the most amazing tattoos all the way up his arms. Snakes and flowers and hearts and a lady in a bikini. He could make her waggle when he moved his muscle.

He showed Biscuits and me and we thought it cooler than cool. We kept wanting him to do it, but Mum gave me a sharp nudge and told me not to keep pestering. She didn't say much else. Kelly's mum said lots and lots. Dad did too.

'I just can't get over the coincidence of you being here on holiday too!' he said. 'I mean, Llanpistyll and Abercoch are such out of the way places.'

'It was our Kelly. She looked them up on the map, she did, and said she just *knew* Llanpistyll would be great. And so we made sure there was a caravan site – and here we are.'

'Oh, you're staying at the caravan site,' said Mum.

'Don't tell me you are too!' said Kelly's mum, laughing and flipping her pony-tail.

Kelly's mum is ever so like Kelly. Only more glittery.

'Oh no! No, we're staying at the Gwesty Bryn Nodfa. It's a very nice quiet family hotel,' said Mum.

'Poor you,' said Kelly. 'It's ever such fun down the caravan site. We've got our *own* amusement arcade and there's swings and all sorts.'

'Yes, it's great for the kiddies,' said Kelly's

mum's boyfriend Dave. 'They can amuse themselves. And we can amuse *our*selves.'

'You must come over. Come now!' Kelly said.

'Can we, Mum?' I said.

'Oh no, dear. No, we're going to look at another castle,' Mum said quickly.

'Then come for tea,' said Kelly.

'Ooh, let's,' said Biscuits.

'No, I'm sorry, we have our evening meal at our hotel,' said Mum.

'*Supper*, then,' said Kelly.

'Please!' I said.

'Double please with knobs on,' said Biscuits.

Mum opened her mouth. It was already in a firm No shape. But guess what!

'*Yes*,' said Dad. 'Yes, we'd love to.'

'But we won't have finished our meal till seven at the earliest,' said Mum. 'And then the boys should really be in bed by half-past seven.'

'You go to bed at half-past *seven*?' said Kelly. 'I don't go to bed till twelve sometimes, isn't that right, Mum?'

'We go to bed *later* than that,' said Dean.

'And this little monkey stays up *all* night sometimes,' said Kelly's mum, picking up Keanu and giving him a little toss in the air.

Keanu squealed and drool came out of his mouth and dripped down onto Kelly's mum.

'You little whatsit!' she said. 'Are you spitting at your mum, eh? I'll give you what for.' She tossed him up in the air again and he squealed and slurped again.

Biscuits and I watched in appalled fascination.

'I don't really reckon babies,' said Biscuits.

'Me too,' I said.

'Me *three*,' said Kelly. 'You try living with one all the time. So – you're coming round to the site, right?'

It was all agreed.

Mum was narked and had words with Dad back at the hotel. Lots and lots of words. We could easily hear them in the next room.

I felt fussed about Biscuits.

'It's OK, Super-Tim,' he said kindly. 'You should hear my mum going on at my dad sometimes.'

I felt a lot better. Though I was a bit worried about going to the caravan site myself.

'Why don't you want to go now? Kelly's your girlfriend, isn't she?' said Biscuits. He made kissy-kissy noises.

'Shut up. I don't *kiss* her.'

'Oh darling Kelly,

You've got such a flat belly,

You're never ever smelly,

Let's sit in the dark and watch telly,' said Biscuits, clasping Dog Hog. He made Dog Hog wiggle around and say in a squeaky voice:

'Oh Tim, Tim,

You're not so dim,

Come and cuddle in.'

'You nut! Shut up, shut up,' I said, seizing Dog Hog and bashing Biscuits on the head with him.

'Ouch! Kelly's attacking me,' Biscuits giggled.

'Well, give it a rest, you pest. Oh no! You've got me doing daft rhymes now. No, about the caravan site. I was thinking . . . what if Prickle-Head and Pinch-Face hang out round there?'

'Ah,' said Biscuits. He smoothed Dog Hog and laid him down gently on his pillow. 'I don't think I'll take him with me then.'

'He can keep Walter company,' I said. 'Biscuits, you were so brave rescuing Dog Hog. I wish I was brave like you.'

'Well, if Prickle-Head threw Walter Bear over the railings you'd go and get him, wouldn't you?' said Biscuits.

'Mmm,' I said doubtfully. 'I *hope* I would. I don't know though. I wish I wasn't such a coward.'

'You're not really,' said Biscuits – but he sounded doubtful too.

'Yes, I am. I'm afraid of everything.'

'Look, *I'm* afraid of Prickle-Head,' said Biscuits. 'And Pinch-Face too. He didn't half dig his nails in when he had hold of me.'

'I'm afraid of heaps of other people too. I even get scared of my dad sometimes.'

'Your dad? That's daft, your dad's smashing. It's your mum who's a bit . . .'

'A bit what?'

'Oh, never mind.'

'OK, I'm not scared of my mum. But I'm scared of all these *things* too.'

'*What* things?' said Biscuits. He pulled a face and made his fingers into scrabbly claws. 'Ghosties and ghoulies?'

'Silly things. Like looking down from the top of the castle. And – and the cracks in the pier. And all sorts of other stuff.' I sighed miserably. 'I'm a complete wimp.'

'You're a tearful wimp – and I'm a cheerful chimp!' said Biscuits, suddenly straddling his legs and letting his arms hang loose. He made loud chimpanzee noises. 'Me want bananas!'

It was impossible to stay depressed around Biscuits.

'Me want bananas too!' I said, and did my own chimp impersonation.

Then we grew into Giant Gorillas and did mating calls and Mum stopped telling Dad off next door to come and tell us off instead.

'You're obviously getting very silly and over-tired already,' she said. 'It's *not* a good idea for us all to traipse over to this caravan site after tea. But as your father has committed us then I suppose we've no option. But we're not going to stay long. We'll just say hello and stop ten minutes to be polite. We certainly won't want any supper.'

'Some of us might!' said Biscuits.

Mum pretended not to hear. She wasn't talking to Dad at all when we drove over to the caravan site. I was a bit quiet myself, still worried that we might meet up with Prickle-Head any moment. I peered round anxiously as we walked down the rows of caravans – and then someone leapt on my back!

'Hey, Tim, it's me!' Kelly said. 'What are you screaming about?'

'You made me jump,' I gasped. 'Don't creep up on me like that again, Kelly.'

'Oh, go on, it's fun,' said Kelly. 'Hi, everyone. Our caravan's at the back, over by the oak trees. This way!'

She directed us like a traffic policeman. A big boy with short hair suddenly ran down the steps of his caravan and I stopped still, my heart thudding – but it wasn't Prickle-Head after all, just some mild mini look-alike.

'Do you know him?' said Kelly. 'He was sucking up to me down the swings last night. But I told him I wasn't interested.'

'Really?' I said, cheering up a little. 'No, I don't know him. But there's this other boy from somewhere round here—'

'A friend of yours, is he?'

'He's a Deadly Enemy, him and his mate. They keep getting us, Biscuits and me.'

'What's he done to you then?'

'Well. First of all he kicked my . . .'

'He *kicked* you?'

'No, he didn't kick me. He kicked my sand-castle.' I felt silly saying it. I sounded like a really little kid. 'It wasn't an ordinary sand-castle. It was a proper motte and bailey castle and I'd spent hours building it. And then they attacked us on the pier. It was really scary, Kelly, I thought they were going to throw us right over into the water. They were teasing Biscuits and they dropped Dog Hog over the railings.'

'But I bet you rescued him like you rescued my Theresa Troll, right?' said Kelly.

'Wrong,' I said. 'I was useless. Biscuits rescued him himself. He was brilliantly brave, Kelly. But even Biscuits is scared of Prickle-Head.'

'Prickle-Head!' said Kelly, snorting. 'Look, don't you worry, Tim. If this Prickle-Head bobs up and starts giving you bother *I'll* sort him out for you, OK?'

'OK,' I said, and we shook hands on it.

We carried on holding hands as we walked over to Kelly's caravan. It felt . . . odd. I've held hands before. Mum's. This was *very* different. It felt OK. Yet I was scared of Biscuits seeing and laughing. And I was scared my palm might get all hot and sweaty. And I was scared to move my fingers about in case Kelly thought I was trying to tickle her but my hand was so rigid it felt like a baseball mitt. *Scared* again.

'That's our caravan,' Kelly yelled, dropping my hand and dancing forward without a second thought.

I wish wish wish I was a person without a second thought. I have *third* thoughts. But for a while *all* my thoughts were absorbed in admiring Kelly's caravan.

It was all so neat and tidy and dinky and perfect, like the best Wendy House in the world. I especially liked the way the table folded up and the bed folded down.

'That's Dean's bed. When he's being a right

pain I shove the bed back into the wall with him inside,' said Kelly.

Even Mum seemed impressed with the proper flushing toilet and the television and the frilly curtains up at the window.

'It's like a little palace,' she said politely.

'And here's my princess,' said Kelly's mum's boyfriend Dave, and he put his arm round Kelly's mum and squeezed her tight.

'Get off of me,' she said, but you could tell she was pleased.

Kelly pulled a *yuck* face at Biscuits and me.

'Do you want a Coke, you two? We've got lots in the fridge.'

'You've even got a fridge!' said Mum.

We all had drinks. Dad and Kelly's mum's boyfriend Dave had a can of beer. Mum said '*No*, thank you' when she got offered a beer too.

'I know what you'd like,' said Kelly's mum.

Mum's eyebrows went up as if she didn't think that very likely.

'I'm not really a drinker,' she murmured, as Kelly's mum produced a bottle of Baileys.

'You try a drop of this,' said Kelly's mum. 'Got a sweet tooth, have you? It tastes just like chocolate.'

'Like chocolate!' said Biscuits. 'Can I have some too?'

Kelly's mum gave him one weeny sip. Mum looked horrified – but when she took an even weenier sip of her own glassful she looked surprised. She didn't say anything, but she drank it all up. *And* had another glass after that.

It seemed to put her in a good mood because she didn't say no when we all ordered take-away pizzas on Kelly's mum's boyfriend Dave's mobile phone.

'I'd never have thought I'd be ordering a pizza in Llanpistyll,' said Dad.

'Well, don't get too excited. We ordered them last night and the first lot went astray,' said Kelly's mum. 'Some of them little toerags waylaid the guy on the pizza-bike. Honestly! Kids nowadays!'

All the grown-ups started in on one of those yawny-yawny kids-of-today conversations while Dean showed us all his toys. I started fooling around with his Lego bricks and made him a little castle.

'Oh wow! That's great, Tim,' said Kelly. 'Make one for me, eh?'

The four of us played with the Lego. Baby Keanu kept trying to smash everything in sight. Then he mistook a red Lego brick for a baby rusk and rammed it in his mouth. He did his best to swallow. He started to turn as red as the brick.

'Keanu's choking,' said Kelly calmly, and she tipped him upside down and thumped him on the back.

The brick came shooting out like a bullet. Keanu crowed happily, none the worse.

'That's some party trick, Kelly,' I said. 'Does he often swallow things?'

'All the time,' said Kelly. 'Hey, I wonder what you were like as a baby, Biscuits! I bet you stuffed *everything* in your little gob. Bricks, rubber dollies, your own little booties . . .'

'His dummy, yum yum, chew chew, swallow! His baby bottle, yum yum, crunch crunch, swallow! Hey, his *pottie*, yum yum *OUCH*!'

Biscuits was doing his best to turn *me* upside down, but mercifully the pizzas arrived just at that moment. We *all* went yum yum, munch munch. We ate outdoors because the caravan was quite a squash with eight and a half people shut inside. Lots of other people were sitting outside their caravans chatting and eating and drinking. Kelly and her family had only arrived yesterday but already everyone knew them. Some kids came over and asked if Kelly was coming over to the swings with them.

'Maybe later. I've got my friends here, see,' said Kelly. 'Isn't that right, Tim?'

'Sure, Kelly,' I said, pleased to be singled out as Kelly's special friend.

Biscuits didn't mind. He was busy with his second pizza.

But then Dad went and spoilt it all.

'Why don't you all play together, eh? How about a game of French cricket? I'll show you how to play if you like.'

'Oh no,' I mumbled. 'Please don't let's play, Dad.'

'I shall get hiccups if I have to play,' said Biscuits, his mouth full.

'I don't want to play with those kids anyway, they're boring,' said Kelly.

Dad didn't listen to any of us. He started careering round looking for a bat and ball. He couldn't find a bat at all and the only ball was a red and yellow stripey one belonging to Keanu. He'd just started the mammoth task of hugging it to his chest and licking it all over and he didn't appreciate Dad taking it. Not one bit.

'There must be an old cricket bat somewhere,' said Dad.

'Sorry, mate. Not my cup of tea, cricket,'

said Kelly's mum's boyfriend Dave.

'What about using my umbrella?' said Kelly's mum, hitching the howling Keanu onto her hip. 'Oh do put a sock in it, young man! Kelly, find my brolly.'

Kelly nipped inside the caravan and came out with a very fancy spotty umbrella. She aimed it at a stone with a nifty little swing.

'Watch it, Kelly! Maybe that umbrella's a bit fragile.'

'Let's play golf instead of cricket,' said Kelly, giving another stone a whack. Then she squealed, her pony-tail waving like a flag as she jumped up and down.

'*I* know! Let's go and play Crazy Golf. Let's, let's, let's!'

'How can you play Crazy Golf now, dear? It's nearly dark,' said Mum, looking at her watch. 'Oh my goodness, we'd better be getting back to the hotel.'

'No, one of the kids on the site told me, you can play it by floodlight. Oh *please*!'

'No, I don't really think—' Mum started.

'Just one quick round. And it's on us,' said Dad.

There'd been a lot of adult argy-bargy about who was paying for the pizzas. Kelly's mum's boyfriend Dave had won. Mum was mega-fussed about it, so she couldn't really back out of the Crazy Golf idea, seeing as it was now our treat.

There was just one problem. One huge enormous disastrous drawback.

'I've never played Crazy Golf!' I said.

'Neither have I – but it's great,' said Kelly.

'Have you played Crazy Golf, Biscuits?' I asked.

'Nope. Like the sound of Crazy. Not too nuts about the Golf bit though,' said Biscuits, easing the waistband on his straining tracksuit trousers.

'We all need a bit of exercise,' said Dad, patting his own tummy. He seized Kelly's mum's umbrella and did a fancy golf swing of his own.

'Oooh, I can see we've got an expert here,' said Kelly's mum, fluttering her eyelashes at him.

Dad gave a silly laugh and then patted baby Keanu on the head. Keanu howled harder.

I felt like howling myself when we got to the Crazy Golf. It was brilliantly lit up by floodlight, with heaps of people playing. The course was huge, with little waterfalls trickling here and there, and all sorts of twisty bits and hidey holes and hillocks. There was a wide wall all the way round the course so that people could peer over and gawp at the golfers.

Dad was a bit taken aback when he saw how much it was, but he said, swallowing hard, that he'd like tickets for seven players, him and Mum, Kelly's mum and Kelly's mum's boyfriend Dave, Kelly herself and Biscuits and me.

'*And me!*' Dean said, outraged. 'Me play too! I can play, can't I, Mum, *can't I?*'

'Of course you can play. Sorry, pal, I just didn't realize you were big enough,' said Dad.

'I'm *ever* so big,' said Dean, standing on tip-toe.

I was huddling up in horror.

'Dad, just get seven tickets. I won't play,' I said.

'What? Of course you're playing, Tim,' said Dad.

'But I don't want to,' I hissed. 'I can't play Crazy Golf. I'll be useless.'

'Don't be silly, Tim. It's *fun*,' said Dad.

Everyone else thought it was fun. We were all given golf clubs, big ones for the grown-ups, middley ones for Biscuits and Kelly and me, and a little one for Dean. He waved it above his head excitedly. It caught me on the chin. It hurt a *lot* but Dad gave me a warning glance and I couldn't say anything much.

177

Kelly had first go and she hit the ball so hard it whizzed right across the first green, hit the wall at the end, and went socking straight back to where she'd started. I went bright red on her behalf but she just laughed.

'That was just a practice shot!' she said, and had another go.

This time her aim was perfect. She hit the ball so that it whizzed up the little slope but slowed down in time so that it stopped almost on the edge of the hole.

'Wow! I'm good at this!' Kelly yelled immodestly.

Her mum was even better. She passed Keanu over to my mum, hardly bothered to take aim, gave the ball a sharp little tap – and got a hole in one!

'Well done, well done!' said Dad, and patted her on the back.

Dave gave her a great-big-kiss-on-the-lips – a very different sort of kiss from the kind Dad gives Mum.

Mum didn't look in a kissy mood at all. She thrust Keanu at Dad and took aim. She didn't get a hole in one. Or two or three or four. Dad kept telling her to hold her club at a different angle and Mum's lips got tighter and her knuckles whiter as she gripped the club and whacked. Her score was six.

Dean scored six too. He did much better than I'd expect of a little kid his age.

Then Kelly's mum's boyfriend Dave had a go and he scored *another* hole in one. There was another great-big-kiss-on-the-lips. They even made *noises*. Biscuits imitated them delightedly. Mum nudged him and frowned. I'd have died of embarrassment if I was Kelly but she just laughed and said if they went on like that she'd have to tip them in the water-fall to cool them off.

Then it was Dad's turn. He still had Keanu. He tried to pass him over to Biscuits and me, but we backed away. Kelly rescued us and took him herself. Dad took a long time, bending his knees and peering at the hole and swinging his club around.

'Come on, mate, get on with it,' Kelly's mum's boyfriend Dave said, wiping Kelly's mum's lipstick off his chin.

Dad looked a little irritated and hit the ball. He didn't get a hole in one. Or two. He scored three.

'Here, I thought you were meant to be an ace golfer!' said Kelly's mum's boyfriend Dave, looking amused.

'Yes, but no-one can play properly on these little Mickey Mouse greens,' Dad said quickly. 'Come on, boys, get a move on. We're holding up the next players.'

I turned round and saw to my horror there was a little queue of people waiting to start their game. They'd all be watching me.

'I don't want to play!' I mumbled.

'You might be good at golf,' said Biscuits cheerily. 'Shall I go next then?'

Biscuits was brilliant! He very nearly got a hole in one himself, but it just bounced over it. He sunk the ball with just one more quick putt.

'Wowie! *I'm* good at golf!' said Biscuits, doing a little joggy up and down dance, making everyone laugh.

I was glad for him – and yet I wished he'd made a real muck-up of it. Then I wouldn't be the worst.

'Come on, Tim,' Dad yelled at me. 'Everyone's waiting.'

'Look, it's OK, I won't play,' I said. 'I don't mind a bit. I don't want to make all these people wait.'

'Don't be so silly, Tim,' said Dad, and he came striding over to me. He lowered his head. 'Don't show me up in front of all the others,' he hissed. 'Just get on with it.'

I tried. My hands were slippy as I seized the club. I took a wild swing. And missed completely.

'Hey, hey, careful!' said Dad. 'No, you've got to keep your eye on the ball. Have another go.'

I tried. I did hit the ball this time. About a centimetre.

'Hit it a bit *harder*, Tim,' said Dad, sighing. 'And hold the club with your hands together. No wonder you're so useless.'

I tried again. I could hear giggling behind me. Kelly and Biscuits were talking together, looking at me.

It was cold in the moonlight, with a sharp breeze off the sea, but I was burning hot. I took another swing and the ball went careering off in totally the wrong direction.

There was a great scornful whoop. Not from behind. Not from in front. From above. I looked up. *It was Prickle-Head and Pinch-Face!*

'Oh no. Oh Dad, please. I can't play any more. Don't make me,' I begged.

'Just do your best,' Dad said.

'But those boys, they're watching me.'

'Take no notice.'

I took another swing. How can you take no notice when your worst enemies in the world are cracking up laughing because you're so hopeless?

Mum started walking towards me, looking cross. Oh no. It was getting even worse.

'You boys up there! You mind your own business!' she shouted.

They hooted even harder. I took one last desperate shot and missed again.

'What a load of rubbish!' yelled Prickle-Head, and then he took his Coke can and threw it at me. 'Rubbish, rubbish, rubbish! Throw your rubbish at the rubbish!'

'*Right!*' said Dad. Kelly's mum's boyfriend Dave was coming over too.

Prickle-Head and Pinch-Face decided to make a run for it.

'But we're still going to *get* you,' Prickle-Head yelled. 'You just w-a-i-t!'

Chapter Five

Tim's diary

I have become an intrepid explorer. Ever so <u>intrepid</u>. I like that word. Biscuits is nowhere near as intrepid as me.

First we went exploring in these ancient caves. But perhaps I was a bit too intrepid. I got horribly injured and needed medical attention.

Then the intrepid exploring team took on a new member. Kelly. And then yet another explorer sustained a disastrous injury. This was Biscuits.

And so Kelly and I did a Mega-Explore, just us two, and we found new undiscovered territory. It was brilliant.

Something very extraordinary happened. I'm not going to say what. Biscuits might just peek in this notebook!

I don't peek. Cheek!
I can rhyme. All the time.
I had sausages and
sausages and sausages
and sausages and
sausages and sausages,
On my breakfast plate,

And one and a half
ice-creams and
my entire emergency
secret biscuit supply
because I was in a state.

Tim is dim
To like smellybelly Kelly.

I went up and up and up the tower steps, gasping for breath. There was someone behind me. I could hear them getting nearer and nearer.

I kept craning back fearfully but it was so dark and I couldn't see anything. But there was a faint glimmer ahead. I was nearly at the top.

I made one last desperate effort and stepped out onto the castle battlements, my hands ready to clasp the wall . . . *but it wasn't there*!

I was standing on a tiny parapet, the wind whistling around me. If I took just one step forward I'd be treading thin air!

'*Where's the wall?*'

There was a horrible laugh from behind

me. I turned my head stiffly, not daring to move any more in case I toppled over.

Prickle-Head was grinning at me from the doorway. He stamped his huge boots.

'These are great for kicking. A few kicks at that wall and it crumbled. You're the one that's going to crumble now, Mummy's Boy. You like cissy pretend games, don't you? Well, you can play at being a weathercock now. Have fun!'

He dodged back and slammed the door shut. I heard the thud and rattle as he bolted it from the inside.

'Please! Come back! You can't do this!' I screamed.

'I *said* I was going to get you,' Prickle-Head shouted from behind the door.

I heard the clump of his boots down and down and down the steps.

I was left, unable to move, my head spinning, eyes streaming, mouth screaming. It was so windy I could barely keep my balance. I had to keep still, it was my only chance, but I was being buffetted from side to side, and I felt so sick and dizzy I couldn't keep my legs stiff. I staggered forward, arms flailing wildly – and then I fell.

Down, down, down . . .

and landed with a bump.

'Tim?'

'Oooh!'

'What're you doing on the floor?'

'I fell out of bed. I think I was having a nightmare.'

'Oh. Right. Night then,' said Biscuits.

Walter Bear had fallen with me. I clutched him tight against my chest.

'Tim?' said Biscuits.

'What?'

'Why aren't you getting back into bed?'

'Because – because I don't want to go back to sleep. In case the nightmare comes back.'

'Was it a really awful maniac-killer-with-a-machine-gun nightmare?' said Biscuits.

'Worse!'

'Wow. Well. Do you want to get in my bed for a bit?'

'Yes please,' I said.

It wasn't very comfortable in Biscuits's bed. Biscuits himself took up a great deal of room, and his sheets were all prickly with crumbs. But it was much much cosier squashed up with him than my own cold bed where the Prickle-Head dream was still lurking, ready to flash on the screen in my head the minute I closed my eyes.

Walter Bear had also crept in with me. He cuddled up with Dog Hog.

'Is Tim feeling better now?' said Dog Hog.

'Much better, thank you,' said Walter.

'He doesn't *sound* much better. Tell him not to worry. It was only a nightmare. It can't come true,' said Dog Hog.

'It can,' said Walter. 'He says it's about Prickle-Head.'

'Ah,' said Dog Hog. '*Him.*'

'Yes,' said Walter Bear. 'He's going to get Tim.'

'And Biscuits,' said Dog Hog.

'He's going to get me *more*,' I said in my ordinary voice, forgetting to be Walter Bear. 'He chased me up this castle and then left me right at the top and there was nothing to hold on to and it was so awful—'

'But he couldn't really do that,' said Biscuits.

'Well, all right. But he could . . .' I paused, thinking of 1001 possibilities.

'He can't do anything really,' said Biscuits firmly. 'Not with your mum and dad around. Especially not your mum.' He chuckled.

I started laughing too, but a little uneasily.

'I suppose he can't actually *kill* me,' I said. 'But – but he can still call me horrible names.'

'We can call him horrible names back,' said Biscuits. 'I know! Let's have a Horrible Names for Prickle-Head contest!'

This was enormous fun. We started off mildly enough:

Pea-brain Prickle-Head.

Pig-manure Prickle-Head.

Pukey Prickle-Head.

Then the names got longer and fancier and much much ruder.

We were soon shaking with laughter, so that we were both in danger of tumbling right out of bed.

Then I suddenly heard a bedroom door slam. Footsteps, rapidly approaching!

'Help!' I hissed, and I shot out of Biscuits's bed and into my own.

'What on *earth* are you two boys playing at!' Mum whispered fiercely, bursting into our room. 'It's four o'clock in the morning and you're waking the whole hotel!'

I kept my eyes shut and tried to breathe evenly, though my heart was thudding. Biscuits gave a very realistic little snore.

'You can't fool me,' said Mum – but she sounded uncertain.

She waited . . . and then we heard her tip-toeing out.

I felt the most desperate giggle shaking my whole body. I had to go down under the sheets to muffle it. Biscuits was snorting too. A little too loudly.

'Sh! She'll come back! We'd better go to sleep now,' I said.

'But I'm wide awake,' said Biscuits. 'And I'm *starving*. I'm going to ask for double sausages at breakfast. *Triple*.'

He did too. Mrs Jones laughed delightedly and called him Little Lord Greedyguts.

'Anything to oblige and fill the Royal Tum,' she said, bustling off to the kitchen.

Biscuits and I laughed too, but Mum frowned. She wasn't in a good mood anyway because of her disturbed night.

'Really, Biscuits! It's very rude of you to keep asking Mrs Jones for more food. She gives you very generous portions as it is. You mustn't do it.'

'But she *likes* it when I ask for more. She thinks it's funny,' Biscuits protested.

'Well, I don't think it's funny at all,' said Mum. 'And you can't possibly want any more sausages. You'll be sick.'

'I'm never sick,' said Biscuits. 'Even on the day I had a Christmas dinner with my mum and dad and then we went to my auntie's and we had another whole Christmas dinner with her and then we went to my gran's in the evening and we had a big buffet and I ate *all* the sausages on sticks, every single one. I wasn't sick then.

And I wasn't even sick on my birthday when—'

'*I'm* getting sick of this subject,' said Mum.

Mrs Jones was coming back with a plate of sizzling sausages, so Mum was forced to smile and be extra grateful.

Biscuits tucked into the sausages. He ate them all. The whole plateful. And then he smacked his lips happily.

'When you die they'll pickle your stomach and doctors will come and look at it and *marvel*,' I said.

Biscuits still looked hopefully at the ice-cream stall as we went on the beach, but after one glance at Mum he could see there was no point asking.

Dad made a great to-do of getting the deckchairs positioned and the windbreak up.

'You're probably wasting your time. It looks as if it's going to start raining,' said Mum, eyeing the grey sky.

'Nonsense!' said Dad. 'The sun's just about to break through, you'll see.'

Mum sniffed, pulled on another cardigan, and got her book out of her beach-bag. Dad reached for his paper, taking great deep breaths to show he was appreciating the balmy air, though there were goose pimples from the end of his shorts to his ankles.

'You two boys had better run about a bit to get warm,' Mum said.

'I'm warm enough,' said Biscuits, getting out his comic.

I read my own comic for a bit, and then I got my drawing book and doodled around doing a picture strip of me and Biscuits being Super-Tim and Biscuits-Boy. Super-Tim swooped up to the castle battlements and rescued damsels in distress who were swooningly grateful. He rounded up evil enemies, conquering them with a swift chop to the chops. 'Kerpow!' said Super-Tim and 'Wow!' said Biscuits-Boy, marvelling at his best friend's bravery and brawn.

'What are you drawing?' said Biscuits, peering over my shoulder.

'Just silly rubbish,' I said, crumpling the page quickly. 'Come on, Biscuits, let's do something. Let's go looking for shells and seaweed and stuff and then identify it from my seaside nature book.'

'That sounds like super fun – *not*!' said Biscuits. 'Just like school.'

'No, we might find something mega-rare. Some extraordinary lugworm all coiled up in the sand and we'll start digging him up and find he's vast, one of the great loathly worms they had in the Middle Ages. Or – or we'll pick up this ordinary old stone and we'll see all the markings on it and it'll be a Stone Age flint used by a caveman to make an axe to attack all the woolly mammoths and sabre-tooth tigers. Aah! I've got a better idea! Let's find a cave and explore it and see if we can find any cave paintings.'

'No, let's find a cave that long-ago pirates used and they hid their ill-gotten gains in it, gold coins and jewels and stuff, and we'll find it in a rotting old trunk and live like lottery winners forever,' said Biscuits.

'OK, OK, well, the cave could have both,' I said. 'Let's find it, eh? Explorers' gear required, Biscuits-Boy.'

'Aye, aye, Super-Tim.'

We got the spades and ran up the beach to where the sand dunes started teetering upwards in an uneven cliff. Little sand-martins flew in and out of an entire birdy housing estate right up at the top. There were a few shallow cubby-holes at the bottom of the cliff, but none that could be seriously described as caves.

'We'll have to tunnel to discover the secret entrance,' I said, attacking the soft sand vigorously with my spade.

'Oh oh! Hard labour time again. Can't you summon up your superhuman powers and blast your way through to save them?' said Biscuits, sitting on the handle of his spade. 'Then I can sit here and have a bit of a rest.'

'You can't have a rest now. You haven't done any work. Come on, let's get digging.'

But as we both set to, Mum started shouting at us. Something about Silly and Dangerous and Stop-it-at-once.

'What's she on about now?' Biscuits muttered. 'Maybe you're not supposed to dig on a full stomach?'

'That's swimming,' I said. 'No, maybe she's worried that we might get sand in our eyes. Actually, I already have, it's all gritty.'

I blinked. Mum loomed large through a hazy blur.

'You *silly* boys! You mustn't *ever* tunnel in sandcliffs like that. It's terribly dangerous. The sand can easily shift and fall on top of you and trap you. Never ever do that. Tim? Why are you screwing up your face like that? Oh darling, have you got sand in your eye?'

She tried making me blow my nose but it didn't work.

'It's OK,' I said, hating the fuss Mum was making in front of Biscuits. 'It's fine now,' I pretended, giving my eye a quick rub with my fist.

This was a serious mistake. My eye

suddenly felt as if it was being scrubbed with emery-paper.

'Oh dear goodness. Hold still, Tim. Oh, your poor eye,' Mum said, as I hopped about in agony, my eye squeezed shut, tears seeping down my cheeks.

'Don't carry on like that, Tim, it's just a speck of sand,' said Dad, coming over. Then he had a proper look. 'Oh dear. It looks like you've got half the beach in there, old son. We need some water to wash it out.'

'I'll get a bucket and get some sea-water,' said Biscuits.

'No, dear – it's salty, that's no use. Come with me, Tim,' said Mum. 'I'll have to take you back to the hotel and we'll use a proper eye bath.'

So Mum whisked me off while Biscuits and Dad stayed on the beach. I tried to stop crying, terrified that Prickle-Head and Pinch-Face might bob up out of nowhere and call me a cissy crybaby, but my eye hurt so much I couldn't help it.

'You poor darling,' Mum said distractedly, as we stumbled across the cabbage field and down the windy footpaths. 'I'll get them to phone for a doctor when we get to the hotel. Or maybe it would be better to dial 999 for an ambulance. You can't be too careful with eyes.

I think you should go to the hospital.'

I started crying harder. By the time we got to the hotel we were both convinced I was going to end up blind in both eyes. Mum was crying too.

'What's the matter. Has the little lad had an accident?' said Mrs Jones. 'Oh dear, sand in his eye, is it? Don't you fret, we'll sort it out in no time.'

She picked me up in her big strong arms as if I were no bigger than baby Keanu. She swept me into her kitchen, sat me down on her draining board, and ran some cold water into a cup. She held it against my hurting eye, tipped my head back, and told me to open the sore eye as wide as possible. It stopped hurting quite so badly. She did it again. It got much better. She had a good peer into my eye, gently holding it wide open.

'Aha! There's one little gritty bit left. We'll get it out in half a tick, you'll see.' She took the corner of her linen tea-towel and gave a quick flick.

'That's it!' she said triumphantly. 'Now, one more rinse for luck and you'll be as right as rain, young man.'

'It's stopped hurting! Well, it's still a bit sore, but it's much much better,' I said, blinking happily.

Mum thanked Mrs Jones again and again. She still felt I should see a doctor to make sure my eye was really all right, but it would mean going all the way to Abercoch to the nearest health centre.

'We don't want to do that, Mum, it would take all morning,' I said.

'We could have a quick look round the shops while we were there. We didn't really get a proper chance last time with your dad and your pal Biscuits.'

'I want to go back on the beach, Mum! Please!'

Mum sighed. 'All right then, dear. But I can't quite see the charm of Llanpistyll beach myself. It's not even sunny enough to get a tan. It's not my idea of fun hunched up in a deckchair hour after hour.'

Mum mumbled and grumbled all the way back to the beach. I raced to the top of the cliff, ready to hurtle down.

'Tim! For goodness sake! Do you want to get *more* sand in that eye? Use the path!'

I stopped listening to Mum. I saw who else was on the beach. Kelly and Kelly's mum and Kelly's mum's boyfriend Dave and Kelly's little brother Dean and Kelly's baby brother Keanu.

'Look who's here, Mum!' I said, and I

charged down the sandy slope, too impatient to bother with the path.

Kelly's mum was sitting in my mum's deckchair beside Dad. Kelly's mum's boyfriend Dave was sitting on the sand with baby Keanu on his lap. Dean was scrunched up in Keanu's buggy pretending to be a baby. Kelly and Biscuits were sitting on a beach towel, Kelly wriggling and pushing, Biscuits refusing to budge. They all had ice-creams. I felt a little left out – and then as I slid nearer I saw Kelly was holding an ice-cream in each hand.

'Hey, Tim! Is your eye better? I was worried when your dad told us. I've saved you an ice-cream anyway,' Kelly shouted. 'Better come quick. Biscuits has been after it!'

'Well, it's all started to melt,' said Biscuits.

'You're an old greedy-guts, you are,' said Kelly, bounding forward to meet me.

She nudged Biscuits a bit in the process. He dropped his own ice-cream in the sand. It was nearly finished anyway, but he gave an immense howl of protest.

I suggested he had half of my ice-cream to make up. I could see it might be a bit difficult to keep things peaceful between Biscuits and Kelly. I liked Biscuits ever so much and I sort of liked Kelly a lot too. I couldn't see why they didn't seem to like each other much.

Mum didn't look at all pleased when she arrived on the beach. She glared at me.

'I told you *not* to go down the sandy way, Tim,' she hissed. Then she smiled, though her lips were very thin and showing too much teeth. 'Well, this is a lovely surprise.'

'Oh, we can't keep our Kelly away from your Tim,' Kelly's mum laughed, still sprawling in Mum's deckchair, her skirt pulled up so she showed a lot of long brown leg.

Mum's smile got even thinner as she sat down heavily on the sand.

'Oh don't sit down! I want you to come with me,' said Kelly's mum. She leapt up and started hopping around, brushing the sand off her feet and stuffing them into strappy little sandals. 'There's meant to be a huge great market this morning in a field the other side of Abercoch. I've been trying to get your old man and mine interested, but you know what men are like when it comes to shopping. But you'll come, won't you?'

'There you are, Mum! You can go shopping after all,' I said, trying to squeeze in between Kelly and Biscuits. It was a terrible squash.

Mum got a bit dithery, but eventually agreed.

'Come along then, children,' she said.

'Oh, we won't take the *kids*. They'll be a terrible bore. The boys hate shopping.'

'Tim enjoys it,' said Mum. 'And I daresay Biscuits will come if there's any food in the offing.'

'Me?' said Biscuits.

'No, let them play on the beach and have fun. The boys might behave themselves but my Kelly will be on and on at me to buy her everything.'

'Me?' said Kelly.

'And Dean *won't* hold my hand and I'm always on pins in case I lose him – and the baby's so grizzly with his teething he's driving me round the bend. No, we'll leave the kids with the men.'

'Oh, I don't think we could do that,' said Mum. 'They'd let them run wild.'

'I daresay!' said Kelly's mum. She linked her arm through my mum's. 'They can have fun and we'll have fun too. Come on. I insist!'

So Mum went off with Kelly's mum. As soon as she started picking her way across the sand Biscuits said, 'Hooray!'

And so did Kelly.

So I did too.

'Now, what are we going to do?' said Kelly. 'Let's explore those rocks over there, right?'

'OK. There might be shrimps,' I said.

'The sort you can eat?' said Biscuits.

'You'd eat *any* sort,' said Kelly scornfully. 'You are a pig, Biscuits. And you've got ice-cream all round your mouth.'

'*You've* got your breakfast orange juice all round yours,' said Biscuits.

Don't be stupid. It's lipstick. My mum's Coral Peach. Honestly!' said Kelly, tossing her pony-tail. 'Come on, Tim.'

I dithered between them. I *wished* they felt more friendly towards each other.

'Where are you three off to?' said Dad.

'We're just going to climb about on those rocks,' said Kelly, giving him a dazzling smile.

'Good idea,' said Dad.

'Me too, me too, me too,' said Dean, trying to climb out of the baby buggy. He tripped over the safety strap and sprawled headlong in the sand.

'Quick!' said Kelly. 'We don't want to get lumbered with him.'

She ran. I ran too. And Biscuits ran, awkwardly, because he'd only had time to put one trainer on.

We got to the rocks at the edge of the beach and started climbing up them. It was quite hard, with big gaps in between the rocks, but I was desperate to show Kelly I could do it. At least I had my trainers on. Biscuits winced and whimpered at every second step.

'You're such a *wimp*, Biscuits,' said Kelly. 'Look, I haven't got shoes on either, have I, but I'm not making a fuss.'

The soles of Kelly's feet were hard and dark and leathery, almost as if she had shoes built into her skin. Biscuits's feet were pale pink and as smooth as satin cushions. Kelly wasn't really being fair.

'*Ouch!*' said Biscuits, stepping on a really spikey rock with his bare foot.

'Try treading on the seaweedy parts, it'll be softer,' I suggested.

It was bad advice. The seaweed was like an oiled slide. Biscuits stepped, slipped, screamed. His arms went up. His legs went up too. He landed very heavily indeed on his bottom.

I felt so sorry for him. But he also looked so funny. Kelly shrieked with laughter. I struggled to stay straight-faced. But Biscuits looked so *comical* sitting in the seaweed. I snorted and then I couldn't stop. I laughed too.

'Oh ha ha ha ha,' said Biscuits sourly.

'I'm sorry, Biscuits,' I spluttered. 'Oh dear, have you hurt yourself?'

'Probably,' said Biscuits, standing up gingerly.

'Are your legs all right? You haven't broken anything?' I asked, patting and prodding him.

Kelly was still laughing.

'Kelly!' I said.

'Look at his shorts! It looks as if he's wet himself!' said Kelly.

'Don't be mean,' I said – but my voice shook. I was very nearly laughing again. The seaweed was very wet and slimy. Biscuits's shorts were wet in the very worst places.

Biscuits stood dripping in his damp shorts. He took Dog Hog out of his pocket and dabbed him dry. Poor Dog Hog had endured several salt-water baths this holiday.

'You could change into your swimming trunks,' I suggested.

Biscuits didn't bother to reply. He gave Dog Hog one last squeeze and then stuffed him back in his sodden pocket. He turned with as much dignity as he could muster, very nearly slipped over again, wobbled dangerously, and then started his descent.

'Oh dear,' I said, watching Biscuits plod across the beach. 'Poor Biscuits. Do you think I should go after him?'

'No! Leave him be. He'll go and eat a biscuit or two – or three or four or five or six – and cheer himself up. It's nice to be without him for a bit. He's worse than our Dean for tagging on when he's not wanted,' said Kelly, climbing again.

'*I* want Biscuits around,' I said.

'Well *I* don't,' said Kelly, as if that settled it. 'Come on, Tim, let's get to the top.'

She hauled me up and up and up. It was getting uncomfortably high.

'Hang on. Look, here's a little rockpool. What's this blobby red thing? I think it's a sea anemone.'

'Mmm,' said Kelly, clearly not interested. She pulled at a few mussels clinging to the rock.

'Don't dislodge them!'

'Are they oysters?' Kelly asked. 'I could do with a pearl to ring the changes with my diamond.'

'Oysters!' I said, sighing. 'Oysters are *completely* different, and they're way down on the sea bed. You have to dive for them.'

'Theresa can dive for them then,' said Kelly, getting her old troll doll out of the pocket of her sweatshirt.

I wished my Walter Bear was little enough to fit in a pocket. Kelly and Biscuits were so lucky to have mascots so discreetly small. I'd need a pocket the size of a shopping bag to accommodate Walter.

Kelly ripped Theresa's dress off and made her dive down into the pool.

204

'Wheee! She likes it, see. She's a great swimmer. Find me some oysters, please, I want some pearls.'

'You don't get pearls in every oyster. They're very rare. Though of course you can farm oysters and have cultivated pearls—'

'Tim,' Kelly interrupted. 'Do you want to be a school teacher when you grow up?'

'Why?'

'Because you don't half *act* like one sometimes.'

'Oh,' I said.

'Oooooooooh!' said Kelly.

I blinked at her. I wondered if she was mocking me. Or playing the fool with Theresa? She scooped her troll out of the little pool and was holding her at arm's length.

'Help! Look what's in her *hair!*' Kelly yelled.

I looked. Then I laughed.

'Oh Kelly. It's just a weeny little crab. Theresa used her hair like a fishing net.'

'Get it *off* her. She doesn't like it,' Kelly said urgently, waggling Theresa frantically.

'Hold her still then. Come here.' I held the little wet troll doll and gently untangled the tiny crab from her long purple locks.

'*Yuck!*' said Kelly, snatching Theresa back and combing her hair with her fingers. 'Poor

poor *poor* Theresa – under mega-attack from a sea monster!'

'It's only a baby crab, Kelly. Nothing to be scared of,' I said, letting the crab scuttle up my arm.

'*I'm* not afraid of it. Theresa is. It practically bit her head off. Ugh, put it back in the water.'

I popped the little crab back into his swimming pool. He paddled out of sight, probably very relieved.

'That's it, you go back to Mummy Crab,' I said.

'*Mummy?*' said Kelly.

She started climbing higher very quickly. I climbed too. I was getting the knack of it now and leapt from rock to rock almost as if I were Super-Tim himself. I felt great (though a bit guilty about Biscuits).

'Wow!' said Kelly, from up above. 'There's an even better beach the other side of these rocks. A little cove.'

It took me a minute or two to get up to the top. Then I saw the beach for myself. It was fantastic, a miniature bay of soft white sand circled by tall cliffs.

'Maybe no-one's ever spotted it before,' said Kelly. 'It looks like you can only reach it by going over the rocks from our beach. Hey, let's get right down there and make it *ours*. We can call it Kelly-and-Tim beach. Come on!'

'Well. Hadn't we better get Biscuits too?'

'No!'

'It's not really fair if we go off without him.'

'He's the one that went off, not us.'

'Yes, but—'

'Look, if we go all the way back to get him and then have to climb back all over the rocks, it'll take forever. Let's just slip down to the beach and claim it – and *then* we'll go back and make friends with him if we must, OK?'

'OK,' I said.

'Great,' said Kelly. She was immediately off like a mountain goat down the other side of the rocks to the perfect private beach.

'Kelly, *wait*. I can't go as fast. And it's all difficult and slippery. Suppose we can't get back up?'

'Of course we'll be able to,' Kelly said, leaping a long way down.

She landed lightly on a flat rock, but it wasn't wedged securely. It wobbled. Kelly wobbled too, but leapt again before she fell. She landed on another lower rock, safely – but only just.

'Kelly! Do be careful. If you slip and break your leg how could I possibly carry you all the way back?' I protested.

'You're such a worryguts, Tim. I'm not *going* to slip,' Kelly shouted.

She leapt.

She landed.

She slipped – and fell.

I screamed.

She grabbed another rock, hung there, stretched one leg to another rock, steadied herself, edged downwards, and stood properly on her two tough feet.

'Kelly! Are you OK?'

'I'm fine.'

'I thought you were going to fall all the way down.'

'I didn't fall at all. I slid that bit on purpose,' Kelly insisted.

But when we both got down to the soft sand I saw a great gash on Kelly's leg.

'You're bleeding!'

'It's nothing,' said Kelly, dabbing her leg impatiently. 'Hey, isn't this beach fantastic? Aren't you pleased I discovered it for you?'

'It's a deep cut, Kelly. You must clean it.'

'Oh Tim, stop fussing. I'm always getting cuts. They're usually far far worse than that. I climbed over a wall with all this broken glass stuck on top once. Look!' Kelly lifted her T-shirt and showed a zig-zag scar across her tummy.

'Gosh!' I said, very impressed.

'I used to kid the guys in my class it was like a zip and I could shove my hand straight into my stomach.'

'You couldn't, could you?'

'No!'

'Well anyway, you ought to go paddling. The sea's salty. It's very healing. My dad had a boil on his bottom once, and he sat in a basin of salty water.'

Kelly snorted with laughter. So did I. We laughed so much we nearly fell over on the sand.

'What a place to have a boil!' said Kelly. 'OK, OK. I'll paddle, just to keep you happy.'

We both paddled. Kelly winced a bit as the water washed over her leg but she didn't complain.

'You're ever so brave, Kelly,' I said.

Kelly beamed at me. A wave splashed high and she jumped to stop her shorts getting wet. Soon we were both holding hands and jumping every wave. We got wet after all but it didn't really matter. Little droplets of water on my eyelashes made me see rainbows everywhere.

'This is our beach, right? We're the only ones who can come here,' said Kelly. 'Let's stake it out as *ours*.'

She searched the sands until she found a big stick. She went near the water's edge where the sand was firm and wrote a message in spiky capital letters.

KELLY-AND-TIM BEACH. PRIVATE. KEEP OUT.

Then she bent over and started drawing a big heart. Well, it was meant to be a heart but it went a bit wobbly and lop-sided. She wrote K L T inside.

'What's it say?' I said. 'Klut? Klot?'

'You're the clot,' said Kelly, pink from bending over. 'It says Kelly Loves Tim. Right?'

'Oh. Right,' I said.

'*Well?*' said Kelly. She held out the stick.

Obediently I drew my own heart and put T L K inside.

'Right!' said Kelly. She came up very close. 'Shut your eyes!' she commanded.

I did as I was told. I felt this quick dab on my cheek. I *think* she kissed me. But when I opened my eyes she'd already darted right across the sand towards the rocks.

Chapter Six

Tim's diary

This was the most <u>terrifying</u> day of my life. Really. I am not exaggerating. Honest. Biscuits almost betrayed me.

I was helplessly trapped and in dreadful danger. And then the Deadly Fiendish Enemy ambushed me. He very, very nearly injured me grievously. <u>Practically</u> <u>murdered me.</u>

My hand is still shaking as I write this.

I am sick of adventures.

This has been the worst yet.

Biscuits was very huffy indeed when Kelly and I climbed back onto the ordinary beach. I kept telling him this and telling him that but he wouldn't answer. I tried cracking some of our extra-funny jokes but he wouldn't even smile.

Kelly absolutely fell about laughing and said 'Oh Tim, you are *funny*.'

Biscuits became even less friendly. He chatted to Kelly's little brother Dean instead. He helped him finish a giant tube of Smarties and in return he built Dean a little boat in the sand just big enough for him to sit in. He encouraged Dean to hold the empty Smarties packet up to his eye like a telescope.

It was a very *basic* boat.

'Shall we make it into a proper boat?' I

suggested. 'What sort of boat do you want it to be? Is it a rowing boat or a sailing boat or maybe a big ocean-going liner?'

'I bet you've done a special project on blooming boats,' said Biscuits. 'It's just a little sand boat for Dean, OK?'

'Yeah. It's my boat, not your boat,' said Dean.

'Leave the little boys with their soppy boats and come and swim, Tim,' said Kelly, trying to pull me away.

I dithered, desperate to keep in with both Biscuits and Kelly. Eventually we all went in for a swim. Kelly's mum's boyfriend Dave even dangled Keanu in up to his ankles.

Kelly was a seriously super swimmer, much better than Biscuits or me. She showed off rather a lot, and kept challenging us to races. She won every time. Biscuits stopped competing. He lay on his back and practised spouting like a whale. I tried too but I couldn't get the knack of spouting. The water went in instead of out and I had a major choking fit. I retreated to the shallows after that and hung around, getting a bit shivery.

I was even more shivery by the time we'd all got out and got dressed.

'We all need to run about and get warm,' said Dad. 'I know. French cricket!'

But luckily my mum and Kelly's mum came back from their trip to the market just then and they'd bought *hot dogs*. They were only lukewarm dogs actually, but they still tasted great, and it stopped Dad banging on about cricket. Even Biscuits cheered up a little – but he looked anxious after he'd eaten his hot dog in three great big bites.

'That's not *lunch*, is it?' he said.

Mum sighed. 'You and your stomach, Biscuits,' she said. But she was in a very good mood after her trip out. She had lots of carrier bags full of shoes and tops and trousers and underwear. She also had *another* carrier full of food.

'Picnic,' she said.

'Is it for us lot too?' said Kelly.

'No Kelly, you know we said we'd find a nice pub with a garden,' said Kelly's mum, trying a new T-shirt on Dave. It had a rude message on it. She'd bought him some new underpants too with an even *ruder* message.

Kelly's mum and Kelly's mum's boyfriend Dave tried to get my mum and dad to go to the pub too. My mum said they were welcome to share our picnic on the beach if they wanted. She seemed much friendlier with Kelly's mum now – though she frowned at Kelly's mum's boyfriend Dave's new naughty underpants.

'There might not be enough picnic to go round,' said Biscuits.

He was very relieved when Kelly's mum and Kelly's mum's boyfriend Dave and Kelly herself and Dean and Keanu all went off to the pub while we stayed on the beach. Kelly wanted to go to the pub for pizza and chips but she was very cross to leave us behind. Well . . . *me*.

'I can come back to see Tim after lunch, can't I?' she said.

'We'll see, pet. We might go on a fishing trip or something,' said Kelly's mum's boyfriend Dave.

'Well, can't Tim come too?' said Kelly.

'He doesn't like fishing,' said Biscuits.

Kelly pulled a face and made a fuss. We could still hear her complaining and arguing halfway down the beach.

'That kiddie isn't half a little madam,' said Mum, dealing out paper plates and little packs of sandwiches.

'She's a sparky little thing though. A cracking swimmer,' said Dad.

'I like her,' I said.

'I don't,' said Biscuits.

We didn't say much else while we ate our picnic lunch. It was banana sandwiches. I particularly like banana sandwiches but I gave

half of mine to Biscuits. And my sausage roll.
And most of my crisps too.

'You're trying to bribe me to be friends,'
said Biscuits.

'Yes,' I said.

'Well. It's working,' said Biscuits.

'Oh Biscuits! Are we really friends again?
Oh *great*!'

'I didn't really break friends. *You* were the
one who laughed at me and went off with
Kelly.'

'I didn't really mean to,' I said.

'I don't know what you *see* in her,' said
Biscuits.

'I don't either,' I said. 'But I do like her. I
like you too! I wish you and Kelly would be
friends.'

'You've got to be joking!' said Biscuits.
'What were you two *doing* all that time over
the rocks?'

'Oh. Just exploring. There's this little
cove.'

'Is it good there? Any pirate caves?'

'I don't really know. We didn't find any.'

'*We* could find some,' said Biscuits, getting
up.

'What, now?'

'Yep. Come on. *We'll* go and explore.'
Biscuits was tying up the laces on his

trainers. 'In the right foot gear this time.' He grabbed his spade. 'Here's my trusty bashing stick in case we encounter any wild animals – or boys.'

'I think you might find it an awful bore getting over all the rocks,' I said.

I didn't know what to do. I so badly wanted Biscuits to stay friends with me. But I wasn't sure I should let him come to Tim-and-Kelly beach. Of course it wasn't *really* our private place. I wouldn't really mind sharing it with Biscuits – but I knew *Kelly* would!

Mum didn't like the idea much either.

'I don't want you clambering over those rocks out of sight. I want you to play here on this beach where we can keep an eye on you.'

'Look, we're not *babies*,' said Biscuits. 'And Tim and Kelly went over the rocks this morning.'

'That was nothing to do with me,' said Mum, glaring at Dad.

'It's not fair if I can't go and explore too,' said Biscuits.

'Hey, *I'll* go with the boys,' said Dad.

So Dad and Biscuits and I set off over the rocks. I just hoped like anything Kelly wouldn't find out. I felt pretty anxious when we got to the top of the rocks because I suddenly remembered the messages we'd left

218

in the sand. There might be some serious teasing.

But the tide had come in. Like a kindly mum with a flannel, the sea had washed the sand clean of all marks.

'Wow! It's a super beach,' said Biscuits.

'We can build a castle now the sand's still wet,' I said.

'You and your castles,' said Biscuits. 'You're like one of them Egyptians wanting a pyramid built, only you haven't got millions of slaves, you've just got me. OK then. Let's get cracking.'

There was just one problem. We only had one spade with us.

'Feel free to use mine, Tim,' said Biscuits, after he'd had three feeble little digs and started a sandcastle the size of a pygmy molehill. Share and share alike.' He handed the spade over with a happy sigh and sat on a rock.

I had a go. A long go. But the sand still wasn't *obedient* enough. I had this splendid vision of a castle in my head but it kept blurring and collapsing in the actual sand.

'Let's dig down and make a big hole instead,' I said giving up.

I started digging. And digging and digging and digging.

Then Dad took a turn. He got very red in the face. He breathed very heavily. Then he straightened up, rubbing his back.

'I'll have to stop, it's doing my back in. I'm going back to Mum. I'll tell her it's perfectly safe for you two boys to play here. You won't go in the sea, will you?'

'No, we're going to dig and see how far down we can go,' I said.

'And you won't try and climb up the cliff?' said Dad.

'*Me?* And Biscuits?' I said. 'Leave it out, Dad.'

'Right. OK then. Have fun digging,' said Dad.

He started climbing back over the rocks, still puffing and blowing.

'It's your turn with the spade, Biscuits,' I said.

Biscuits puffed a lot too. And blew. He leant on the spade.

'Isn't it big enough now?'

'No! We're not even properly down to the dark sand yet.'

'And what's going to happen when we dig through that? We'll come out in Australia and everyone will talk like *Neighbours* and we'll have koala bears and kangaroos jumping all round us.'

'Of *course* we couldn't ever get to Australia! Don't you know anything? Honestly, Biscuits, you're so silly sometimes. We'd have to get right through the Earth's crust and you can't do that, and then you'd go into the core and that's boiling-boiling-boiling hot and—'

'And I feel boiling-boiling-boiling hot right this minute,' said Biscuits. He looked at the hole. He looked at me. 'I know. Get in it, Tim. And sit down.'

'Like this?' I did what he said, puzzled. 'Biscuits? What are you doing? Oh, don't start filling it in!'

'I'm making you a boat, right?'

'Wrong!' I said. I'd wanted to dig the biggest hole ever and see all the different layers of sand and work out how far down they went. I didn't want to mess about playing baby-boats. But I *did* want Biscuits to stay friends. So I sighed and gave up on the idea of Huge Hole.

'OK, OK, I'm in a boat,' I said, and I even helped Biscuits heap the sand back into the hole around me. And on top of me.

'Not on my legs!'

'Yes. Go on. It's more fun like that.' He piled sand up on my lap.

'It's going to look like the boat's sinking,' I said. 'Watch the edge of that spade, Biscuits!'

'Sorry, sorry!' He put the spade down and started patting the damp sand into place.

It felt very heavy, almost uncomfortably so. I tried to shift my legs but they were already firmly stuck under the sand. I tried a violent kick and just about managed to crack the sand above my toes.

'Don't!' said Biscuits, and he got wetter sand and patted it hard.

It set like concrete.

'It's *heavy*,' I said.

'Well keep still,' said Biscuits, piling more sand on.

I tried to push it away but Biscuits took the spade and shovelled hard. My arms got covered. I was stuck.

'This isn't a boat. Not unless it's a submarine,' I said.

'Up periscope,' said Biscuits, heaping more sand right under my chin.

'Biscuits! Let me out now. I don't want to play Boats any more.'

'This isn't Playing Boats. This is the Burying Tim game,' said Biscuits, patting and smoothing the sand harder and harder.

'Oh ha ha,' I said.

Though it didn't feel very funny. I didn't like being stuck there in the sand like that, with just my head sticking out.

Biscuits was panting with effort by now. He stopped and straightened up, wiping his wet brow. He looked at me, his head on one side.

'There! You're done now,' he said.

'Thank goodness. OK. Let me out then. Biscuits? Biscuits!'

Biscuits had started to walk away!

'Biscuits, come back!'

'What's that?' said Biscuits, turning and cupping his ear as if he couldn't quite hear me.

'Biscuits, please! Don't mess about.'

'What's the matter?'

'Don't be *silly*!'

'Ah. That's me. Silly,' said Biscuits. 'Only I'm not the one stuck up to my neck in sand. *You* are. Even though you're so clever.'

'Oh, Biscuits. Don't be like that. Look, get me *out*. It's stopped being a joke. It's not funny at all.'

'I think it's *ever* so funny. Bye, Tim!' said Biscuits, and he started a lumbering run towards the rocks.

'Biscuits! Look, you're not frightening me. It's just your stupid joke. It's very very *boring*. So let's get it over with, right?'

Biscuits didn't seem to be listening. He started clambering over the rocks.

'I don't care a bit,' I said. 'I know you just want me to shout after you.'

He didn't turn round.

He climbed to the top and then started going down the other side. Then he dropped down. And disappeared.

'*Biscuits!*' I shouted.

A gull screamed back at me overhead.

Biscuits had gone. I was all on my own. Stuck up to my neck on a deserted beach. My heart went bang bang bang inside my chest. The gull cried again, swooping low, so that I could see its cruel yellow beak.

I shut my eyes quick.

'Go away!' I said.

It was meant to be a shout but it came out as a feeble whisper.

I waited. My eyes were getting watery behind their lids. When I dared open them tears spilled down my cheeks. I blinked hard. I didn't want Biscuits to catch me crying when he came back.

If he came back.

Of course he'd come back. Or Mum and Dad would come looking for me. Eventually.

There was nothing to cry about. The gull had flown away. It hadn't mistaken me for a juicy fish. I was fine. I couldn't come to any harm even though I was trapped.

I tried to calm myself by staring out to sea. Then I watched the waves. Was the tide coming in or out? I couldn't remember! What if the tide was coming in – rapidly? Suppose it started lapping right around my sand prison, the waves splashing over my head?

I tried kicking madly and thrusting my arms up but the sand was set too hard. It wouldn't budge. I couldn't even make the tiniest crack in it now.

'Oh Biscuits, come back!' I cried. 'Please! It's not a joke any more! I'm frightened.'

Then I heard noises up above me, from right up on the clifftop. I tried to peer round to see who was there but my neck was so packed with sand that I couldn't even swivel my head properly. I heard bumps and thumps. It sounded as if someone was climbing down the cliffs.

'Is that you, Biscuits?' I shouted.

Was this all part of his joke? I couldn't believe he could have scooted up the path to the clifftop so quickly. And surely old Biscuits wouldn't risk his neck climbing down the sheer cliff face? (Though he had been pretty good at abseiling.)

'*Biscuits?*' I yelled, as the sliding and slithering progressed downwards behind me.

Then I saw a head bob up from behind the

rocks. It was munching on a chocolate bar.

'Ha ha! I *really* got you worried, didn't I?' he yelled. 'I didn't really leave you, I just hid behind the rocks.'

'Biscuits?' I said. 'Then who . . . ?'

I tried to crane round again.

I saw Biscuits stop and look behind me. His hand stopped in mid air, holding the chocolate. His mouth stayed open and empty.

I knew it was seriously bad news for Biscuits to forget to eat. My heart was banging to bursting point now. I had a sudden terrible premonition.

Someone started to give triumphant Tarzan whoops as he got nearer and nearer. I could feel my trapped skin erupting in goose-bumps.

Then I heard a thump thump as two very big boots jumped onto the sand.

I saw Biscuits mouth one terrible word.

Prickle-Head.

'Aha! Who have we got here?' he yelled triumphantly. 'Fun time!'

Biscuits was still standing statue-still. Then he moved. I wouldn't have blamed him for one minute if he'd clambered back over the rocks to the other beach. I think I might have done. And he could always say he was rushing off to get my dad.

But Biscuits didn't run away and really abandon me. He started running towards me, spade at the ready, all set to dig me out and rescue me.

But he didn't have time. Prickle-Head got to me first.

'What's this weird little squashy thing in the sand?' he said. 'Is it a little jellyfish?' He put his great boot right on top of my head, pressing down hard enough to hurt.

'Get off!' I said.

'Oooh! The jellyfish can talk! Yuck, it really *is* a jellyfish, there's slime and snot all over its face.'

I sniffed desperately.

'Oh my, it's not a jellyfish at all, it's the little Mummy's boy. What's happened to its weedy wimpy little body then? Someone's chopped its head off. Well, it's no use to anyone. Might as well use it as a football, eh?' He took his boot off my head and took aim.

'Don't you dare kick him!' Biscuits yelled, and he started whirling the spade in a threatening manner.

But Prickle-Head was bigger and quicker. He dodged, pushed and grabbed.

Biscuits ended up on his bottom.

Prickle-Head ended up with the spade.

'Aha! It's *my* turn to play sandcastles now,'

said Prickle-Head. 'Here's a nice castle. Ready-made, couldn't be better. Hey, look at my castle, Rick.'

There was another thump on the sand behind me. Prickle-Head had reinforcements.

Pinch-Face came running into my view. He laughed and aimed a kick at my head. He missed – but only just. I tried to dodge and jarred all down my back.

'Yeah, I don't like that wet blobby bit on top of the castle. Spoils it, doesn't it? So shall I pat it smooth, eh?' Prickle-Head held the spade high and then brought it down hard and fast.

I screamed.

Biscuits leapt up and tried to rugby tackle Prickle-Head. The spade swung and landed with a loud bang on the tightly-packed sand.

'Get *off*, Fatboy,' said Prickle-Head, and he punched Biscuits in the stomach.

Biscuits made a sad little 'oooof' sound, and sank into the sand like a burst balloon.

'Now, let's play Hit the Head,' said Prickle-Head, grabbing the spade again.

'Sounds like fun, Boss,' said Pinch-Face.

'Look, if you really hit me with that you could easily *kill* me,' I said desperately.

'Ooooh! Mummy's boy is getting really

scared now. I bet he's wetting his little panties,' said Prickle-Head.

'*Why* do you want to be so hateful? I haven't done anything to you,' I said, snuffling hard.

'It's fun,' said Prickle-Head. 'Right. I'll take aim.' He raised the spade high above my head. 'And then I'm going to go WHACK!'

'Hey, Boss,' said Pinch-Face. 'You're not *really* going to?'

'What? Are you chicken or something?'

'Of course not. It's just like the cissy said. You could really smash his head in,' Pinch-Face said. 'You're just kidding, aren't you?'

'Am I?' said Prickle-Head. 'You just wait and see. Right. One, two, three . . .'

He waved the spade above his head, his face contorted with effort. I stared up into his eyes. I didn't know if he was really going to do it or not. Maybe he didn't even know either.

'Please don't!' I begged.

But that just made him grin.

'Ready steady *GO*!'

'Hey! You! Stop that! Get away from my boy!'

It was Dad, over at the rocks, scrambling down, the other spade in his hand.

Prickle-Head waved the spade in mid-air.

'Hey, Boss, we'd better scarper,' said Pinch-Face.

He started running.

Prickle-Head whirled the spade one last time and then threw it as far as he could. Then he ran too.

'Oh, Tim!' Biscuits gasped, still rolled up in a ball clutching his stomach. 'Are you all right?'

'Oh, Biscuits!' I said. 'Are *you* all right?'

We both felt very wrong indeed. I cried a bit. And so did Biscuits. And then Dad got to us and dug me out, and rubbed Biscuits's tummy, and gave us both a big hug.

'I couldn't believe my eyes!' he said. 'Thank goodness I decided to bring you the other spade. How dare those boys behave like that!' He waved his fist at Prickle-Head and Pinch-Face who were scrambling up the cliff.

'You stupid bullying little thugs! And you're mad to be climbing that cliff. You'll break your necks – and it'll serve you right.'

Prickle-Head yelled a very rude word at Dad.

'Just wait till I find out exactly who that lad is,' said Dad. 'I've a good mind to go to the local police. That wasn't childish rough play – that was atrocious bullying. Imagine burying you in the sand like that, Tim! How did he do it? Didn't you struggle?'

I hesitated.

'Mm. *I* actually buried Tim in the sand,' said Biscuits.

'*You* did, Biscuits?' said Dad. 'Good Heavens! Why? Tim's your friend.'

'I know. It was just a silly joke. I wasn't really going to leave him like that. I just hid for a minute. But then Prickle-Head came down the cliffs—'

'Biscuits tried to stop him,' I said. 'He was very brave.'

'It was still my fault you were stuck there and couldn't run away from him,' said Biscuits. 'What's your mum going to say when she finds out?'

We all three thought about Mum.

'Ah,' said Dad. 'Well. Seeing as there's no lasting harm done . . . shall us men keep quiet about it? We don't want to worry your mum, Tim. You know what she's like.'

'Yes,' I said.

'*Yes!*' said Biscuits.

'So, if we dust you both down, and mop you up a bit, Mum won't need to know. But I'm still in two minds whether to go to the police or not. Or if I could track down where the boy is staying I could have a serious word with his father.'

We saw Prickle-Head that evening when we went to a fun fair with Kelly and Kelly's mum and Kelly's mum's boyfriend Dave and Kelly's little brother Dean and Kelly's baby brother Keanu.

Prickle-Head was there with *his* mum and his dad and several pricklet brothers and sisters. They all looked almost as fierce and frightening as their big brother Prickle-Head. His *mum* looked fierce and frightening too. She was shouting at the older children. Then Prickle-Head's dad whacked them hard about the head. He gave Prickle-Head a couple of extra smacks. Prickle-Head's dad looked far far far fiercer and more frightening than Prickle-Head.

Dad decided that he wouldn't have a serious word with him after all.

Chapter Seven

Tim's diary

Wow.

And **Wow** again.

WOW WOW WOW!!!

I have had my biggest adventure yet!

Biscuits's diary

We went out to celebrate. Me and my mate Super Tim. And his mum and dad. And that Kelly and her mum and Dave and Dean and Keanu. That lot wanted to celebrate down the pub but Tim's mum suggested an ICE-CREAM PARLOUR

I have to admit this was a truly WICKED idea.

You will never ever guess what Tim had. And he could have had anything. He chose a strawberry ice-cream. Not even a double scoop. Honestly! He might be Super-Tim but he's Weedy-Feedy when it comes to eating. → BORING!

Kelly had a knickerbocker Glory →

I had a Chocolate Biscuit Choo-choo Special. It was an entire packet of milk chocolate digestive biscuits sandwiched together with chocolate ice-cream to make a train, with chocolate buttons for wheels, a Cadbury's Flake for a funnel with a huge plume of cream billowing out like smoke.

It said it was suitable for six portions on the menu. Guess what. I ate it all up myself. And it was YUMMY.

Kelly was barely talking to me. Biscuits had told her about our last desperate encounter with Prickle-Head.

'You took Biscuits to our beach?' Kelly cried indignantly. 'You rat. You total traitorous flea-ridden slimy-tailed rotten rat!'

She kept repeating this, with yet more ratty embellishments, all the while we told her about our narrow escape.

'Do shut it, Kelly. You don't own the beach,' said Biscuits. 'Don't you realize, I got beaten to a pulp and Tim practically got his head bashed in.'

'The way Prickle-Head was holding the spade it could have sliced off the top of my head just like a boiled egg!' I said dramatically.

Kelly refused to be impressed.

'If I'd caught you there with Biscuits I'd have jumped up and down on your head myself,' she said darkly.

She waved Theresa Troll in the air and hit me hard before I had time to duck. It was surprising how much a plastic troll could hurt.

'*Ouch!*' I said, reeling. I had to try very very hard not to cry.

'Serves you right,' said Kelly. 'Just be glad Theresa's not a sharp spade. I'm not like this stupid Prickle-Head you keep going on about. I don't miss when I take aim.'

She stalked off, her pony-tail switching furiously right and left.

'Wow!' said Biscuits. 'Old Killer-Kelly, eh? I dropped you in it there all right, didn't I, Super-Tim?'

'Too right, Biscuits-Boy,' I said, rubbing my head ruefully.

I sighed. At least I was back being friends with Biscuits. I hoped that Kelly might have got over her mega-huff by tomorrow. I so wanted us *all* to be friends.

'What's up, dear?' said Mum, coming and putting her arm round me. 'You're looking a bit peaky. How's your poor old eye? It's not still smarting, is it? It looks a bit watery.'

'It's fine, Mum, really,' I said.

'It's silly, everyone thinks sandy beaches are so safe – and yet they can cause all sorts of problems,' said Mum.

'I know,' I said. I wondered what Mum would say if she knew of my problems in the sand with Prickle-Head.

'I'd be happy to give the beach a miss tomorrow,' said Mum, keeping her voice down. 'We could go for a car trip, maybe explore another castle. You'd like that, wouldn't you, Tim? And Biscuits will go along with that so long as we feed him every five minutes.' Mum sniffed.

'You bet I will,' said Biscuits, who had sharp ears.

'So it's all settled,' said Mum. 'We'll go on a car trip, just the four of us.'

'What's that?' said Dad, coming over. 'Not tomorrow. It's the Caravan Site Carnival Day and we've all been invited, remember?'

'Oh yes,' said Mum. 'But Tim and Biscuits want to go for a car ride, don't you boys?'

'I'd sooner go to a carnival,' said Biscuits. I saw the dreamy look in his eyes. Carnivals meant ice-creams and candy floss and hot dogs.

'What about you, Tim?' said Mum.

I hesitated. I hated to upset her. But if I didn't go to this Carnival Day I knew I'd upset

Kelly even more. I rubbed the sore place on my forehead where Theresa Troll had clouted me.

'I'd like to go to the Carnival Day too,' I said.

It was a BIG mistake.

The moment we got to the caravan site and saw the ropes and flags set out across the beach I realized something terrible.

There were going to be sports.

I am the least sporty boy ever.

'Great!' said Dad, reading the poster. 'There's going to be all sorts of races. Sprinting, relay, three-legged, sack race, egg and spoon. You boys must have a go.'

'It'll be just for people staying at the caravan site,' I said quickly. 'We can't enter, it wouldn't be fair.'

'Don't be such a wimp, Tim,' Dad said sharply. 'Of course you can enter.'

'But I don't want to!' I said.

'Nor do I, actually,' said Biscuits loyally.

'There! We'd have all been much better off if we'd gone for a car ride,' said Mum. 'In fact, why don't we still go? This carnival doesn't look very exciting. There aren't any craft or bric-a-brac stalls, and the tombola prizes don't look much cop. There aren't even many food stalls.'

'Yes, let's go for a car ride,' said Biscuits.

Dad looked exasperated.

'But all Kelly's family are expecting us.'

'I think we've seen a little too much of Kelly's family this holiday,' Mum muttered.

'Yes, I like it best when it's just us,' said Biscuits.

Mum blinked at Biscuits – and then offered him a piece of chocolate out of her handbag to cement their new alliance.

'Tim, you want to see Kelly, don't you?' said Dad.

I dithered. Perhaps there wasn't much point seeing Kelly at the moment, seeing as she wasn't speaking to me. It would be a bit like watching telly with the sound turned down.

'Well . . .'

I heard someone shouting through a megaphone.

'Come and enter for the first race of the day, folks!'

'I want to go on a car trip,' I said.

Mum smiled.

Biscuits smiled.

Dad frowned. But it was three against one so we turned round and started walking away from the caravan site.

'Hey, Tim! TIM! TIM!!'

It was Kelly. She was speaking to me again. She didn't need a megaphone. She had her volume turned right up to maximum force.

'Pretend you haven't heard her,' said Biscuits.

It was not a sensible suggestion. People covered their ears the length of the Welsh coast and said 'That's Kelly!' Cattle in the meadows were mooing 'That's Kelly!' Sheep up in the mountains were baaing 'That's Kelly!' Dolphins and whales way out in the ocean were spouting 'That's Kelly!' Little green men in flying saucers were twitching their antennae and mumbling in Martian 'That's Kelly!'

I turned. We all turned.

Kelly came charging up to us.

'Where are you *going*? The carnival's over on the clifftop. Come on, they've just announced the first race. It's the under-five fifty-steps toddle and our Dean's going to walk it, you watch!'

'I'm sure he will, dear. But we were actually wondering whether to give all these races a miss,' said Mum.

'You can't. I've entered all of you,' said Kelly.

'What?' I said.

'You're doing the three-legged race with me, Tim. Come *on* in case it's next,' Kelly commanded.

'That's it, Kelly, you get this lazy lot organized,' said Dad.

'I've entered you in the dads' race. And there's a knobbly knees contest too. You're down for that and all,' said Kelly.

'Knobbly knees!' said Dad, looking down his shorts at his legs. 'I haven't *got* knobbly knees, young woman.'

'Well, there's a hairiest leg contest too. Would you sooner go in for that?' said Kelly.

'Cheek!' said Dad.

'I told you those shorts were a mistake,' said Mum, sniggering. 'It'll be funny if you win!'

'You might win too,' said Kelly, smiling at her.

Mum blinked. 'Kelly,' she said, very slowly and ominously. 'What have you entered me for?'

'Well, the mums' race, of course. And the Fabulous Forty-Plus Beauty Contest.'

Mum snorted.

Dad snorted too.

'Kelly!' said Mum. 'I am *not* forty-plus.'

'Oh well, never mind,' said Kelly. 'You've a good chance of winning it then, haven't you?

241

Come *on*, we must get a move on or we'll miss Dean's race.'

So we got a move on.

You simply can't argue with Kelly. She's like a steamroller.

'I shall go in for the sack race,' Biscuits muttered. 'And I shall try hard to barge into Kelly. And I shall knock her over. And jump on her. Hard.'

But I could tell his heart wasn't in it. Biscuits was twice Kelly's fighting weight but he knew he'd never get the better of her.

He cheered up a little watching Dean's race. He had got quite matey with him during their boat-building session. Dean wasn't the oldest and he wasn't the biggest under-five by any means but it was obvious he was taking the race very seriously. Most of the kids were fidgetting or talking or whimpering or waving at their mums as they lined up at the starting post on the grass. One or two were facing the wrong way. They had to be turned round quickly or they might have gone hurtling towards the cliff edge and hurled themselves over the top like lemmings. But Dean was clearly concentrating, his teeth gritted, his fists clenched. When someone shouted 'One two three – go!' Dean was off like a shot, charging along, his elbows flapping like little wings. One big kid tripped over just in front of him. Dean ran straight over him, never pausing.

'That's it, our Dean!' Kelly yelled.

'Go for it, Dean!' Biscuits yelled.

'Come on, Dean!' Kelly's mum yelled, standing just beyond the finishing post, holding out her arms to him.

Dean won.

Kelly and Kelly's mum and Kelly's mum's boyfriend Dave and my mum and my dad and Biscuits and me all cheered. Baby Keanu, perched up on Dave's shoulders, gave a cheery sort of chirp.

Dean was given a winner's badge and a little bar of chocolate.

'Wow!' said Biscuits. 'I didn't know they gave you *chocolate*. Hey Dean, are you going in for the three-legged race? How's about you teaming up with me, eh?'

Dean was pleased to be partners with his new pal Biscuits but their pairing wasn't very successful. Dean was little but ran very fast. Biscuits was big but ran very slowly. They fell over. They fell over again. And again. And then Biscuits tried picking Dean up and carrying him, still with their legs tied together. And then they fell over again because they were laughing so much. Luckily

Biscuits was so well padded he didn't hurt himself at all and Dean always managed to land on top of Biscuits so it was just like bouncing on a huge well-stuffed sofa.

Kelly and I didn't do much better.

My heart sank as she tied our legs together with her mum's scarf. She did it so tightly she cut off all the blood supply to my foot. She looked very determined. Kelly liked to win.

I would have liked to win too. But I knew we didn't have a chance.

I tried hard to get ready, get steady and go.

'Run!' Kelly commanded.

I ran. She ran. But not together.

We tripped over. It hurt rather a lot. I wondered if I ought to stay lying there on the grass.

'Get up!' Kelly squealed.

I decided to get up. I was barely on my feet before Kelly tore off again. I staggered along beside her for three or four paces, and then tripped again.

'Oh Tim, you're so *useless*!' Kelly yelled.

I agreed with her meekly.

'Look, shut up and get up,' Kelly said sharply.

I tried to do as I was told.

It didn't work.

We were last in the three-legged race. We didn't actually finish. Kelly tore the scarf off our legs and stormed off. I was left to limp the rest of the way to the finishing post by myself with everyone laughing at me. I saw Kelly's mum and Kelly's mum's boyfriend Dave pretending not to have noticed. I saw Mum's face. I saw *Dad*. I felt so awful. Then I heard another loud braying laugh and a cry of, 'Mummy's boy!'

Prickle-Head.

I felt even worse.

But Dad looked up. He'd heard the laugh too. Prickle-Head didn't have *his* dad with him this time, only Pinch-Face. Pinch-Face saw my dad looking suddenly fierce. He said something to Prickle-Head. They both scooted off sharpish.

I felt a fraction better. But *only* a fraction.

'Cheer up, Tim,' Biscuits said. 'Dean and me were hopeless too. They laughed at us and all.'

But Biscuits had learned the knack of making people laugh *with* him. They laughed *at* me.

'I'm ever so sorry, Kelly,' I said humbly.

Kelly raised her eyebrows and sighed.

'So I should think!'

'You be quiet, our Kelly. Tim did his best,'

said Kelly's mum. 'You were the mean one, rushing off like that and leaving him on his own. Anyway, it's only a bit of fun, kids.'

'That's right,' my mum said gratefully.

Dad didn't say anything.

I knew he thought I was useless too.

I tried hard not to mind too much as the races went on and on. Nobody made me go in for anything else. But it didn't matter. I cheered Kelly and Dean in all their running races. They won. I cheered Biscuits in his sack race. He didn't win but he bounced along grinning all over his face so that everyone clapped nevertheless. I was pleased for him. But I still minded and minded about me inside.

Then the dads had a race. My dad ran like crazy and went purple in the face. Kelly's mum's boyfriend Dave ran like he was hardly bothering. And won.

My dad congratulated him but I could see he minded a lot.

Then it was the mums' race.

'I'm not going in for it,' said my mum.

'Go on, it'll be a laugh,' said Kelly's mum.

There was nothing going to stop *her* going in for it, even though she didn't have the right sort of shoes to run in, just backless sandals with heels. She gave them to Kelly to hold and went to the starting post, practically dragging my mum with her.

I saw my mum's face.

I realized she hated sports just the way I did. She especially hated the idea of running in front of everyone and looking stupid. I felt a horrid new squeezing in my tummy. My mum was plumper than the other mums. And I'd seen her running for a bus. Her legs kicked out at the sides and her bottom waggled. I didn't want to see everyone laughing at Mum.

'This is going to be a laugh,' said Biscuits.

Then he saw my face.

'Hey, your dad gave you some pocket money, didn't he? Let's go and get an ice-cream from the van over there,' Biscuits suggested.

'OK.' I looked over at Kelly who was prancing around in her mum's high heels.

'Not her,' Biscuits said quickly. 'Just you and me.'

So we sloped off together while everyone else was waiting for the start of the mums' race. We bought an ice-cream each and stood licking them at the edge of the cliff.

We heard great shrieks and roars and laughing behind us.

I winced.

'Hey, let's have our own private Super-Tim

and Biscuits-Boy race,' said Biscuits, swallowing the rest of his ice-cream whole. 'We'll have a roly-poly-down-the-sand-to-the-beach race, right?'

'Right!' I said, and then I stepped over the edge and started rolling right away.

'Hey! Cheat! I didn't say go!' said Biscuits behind me, as he hurled himself over the edge of the beach too.

I went roly-poly roly-poly roly-poly over and over and over, my eyes squeezed shut to stop any more sand getting in them. I bumped a few bits and went very wobbly but it was still fun, if scary. And I landed on the beach first.

'I won!' I said as I landed bump on my bottom on the beach.

'Look who it isn't! Old Mummy's boy!' came a dreadfully familiar voice.

But it sounded odd. Hollow. Sort of echoey and far away.

I blinked. I couldn't see Prickle-Head anywhere. Then I realized. He was in one of the sandy caves, burrowing away. I saw his great big boots and Pinch-Face's trainers sticking out.

I decided it would be wise to hasten back *up* the cliff sharpish.

'I'm second!' Biscuits shouted above me,

hurtling down in a great flurry of sand.

He was sliding down with great thumps and bumps. And suddenly the sand all around him started shaking.

I stared. And then I shouted, 'Get out the cave quick! The cliff is giving way! The sand's all sliding!

Pinch-Face backed out so quickly that Biscuits couldn't steer past him and landed bang on top of him. They sprawled in a heap, Pinch-Face groaning, Biscuits giggling.

'Where's Prickle-Head?' I said. 'Did he get out too?'

'Must have done,' said Pinch-Face, picking himself up.

There was a huge mound of new sand down on the beach.

'Wow! I caused a landslide,' said Biscuits, looking at the sifted sand. 'No, a *sand*slide!'

I stared. Something glittered in the sand. A stud. Several studs. Prickle-Head's boots! He was buried in the sand!

'Quick!' I said. 'We've got to get him out. Dig, you two. Come *on*. He's buried alive under all that sand. He'll die if we don't dig him free.

I hated Prickle-Head but I didn't want him to *die*. We scraped and scrabbled at the sand covering him.

'Do his head end so he can breathe,' I said, but when we tugged his top half free his head lolled. His eyes were shut. I bent my own head nearer. He wasn't breathing.

'He's dead!' said Pinch-Face.

'I've murdered him with my landslide!' said Biscuits. 'Oh help, oh help, oh help, oh help.'

'Run and *get* help, what'syourname, Rick, *quick*!' I yelled. 'Biscuits, stop it! Keep getting the sand off him. Maybe that's stopping his breathing. It's crushing his chest.'

'He's dead already, I just know he is!' Biscuits gasped, clasping Prickle-Head's horribly lolling head.

It suddenly reminded me of floppy old Dog Hog and the game we'd played in the car together on the way to Llanpistyll.

'Artificial respiration!' I said. 'Quick, Biscuits, do it!'

'I don't know how!'

'You did it with Dog Hog and Walter Bear.'

'I was just messing about. Oh Tim. He *is* dead.'

'Then I'll have a go at this kiss of life thing,' I said, as Biscuits scraped more sand off Prickle-Head.

I tilted his head back further so I could get at his mouth properly.

'Breathe into it then!' said Biscuits.

'No, wait,' I said, seeing all the sand around Prickle-Head's mouth. I shoved it open with my fingers and scooped lots of spitty sand out.

'Is he breathing now?' said Biscuits.

'Not yet.'

I stared at Prickle-Head's face, wondering how to do it. I need the mouth to stay open – and my breath to get down inside him. I pinched his nose to stop the air getting out, took a deep breath, and then breathed quickly into Prickle-Head's mouth. Then I took another breath and did it again. And again. And again.

Biscuits kept scrabbling all the while, clearing the sand.

I breathed and breathed and breathed.

'It's not working,' Biscuits wept.

I went on breathing into Prickle-Head.

I breathed again and again and again.

Prickle-Head suddenly coughed.

I shot up from him. Prickle-Head turned his head sideways.

'He's being sick. Yuck!' said Biscuits.

'He's *alive*!' I said.

'Oh Tim! He *is* alive. I'm not a murderer after all. And you're a *hero*!' said Biscuits.

And then lots of people came running

down the zig-zag path and more sand started sliding, so Biscuits and I dragged Prickle-Head completely free. We were surrounded by people and there was noise and pushing and questions – and then suddenly someone came charging through everyone, running even faster than Kelly. It was my mum!

She picked me right up and hugged me hard.

'Oh Tim! I thought it was you who'd been buried! Oh thank God you're safe. And Biscuits is too?'

'Mum! Put me down! People are *looking*.'

'I'm fine. And I do hope Prickle-Head is. Tim saved him. He gave him the kiss of life. He was wonderful!' said Biscuits. 'He's a hero!'

'Tim! Wow! You saved his *life*? What did you do that for? I thought you didn't like him!' said Kelly barging through everyone. 'Still, you *are* a hero. My boyfriend Tim's a hero.'

'Oh son! Did you really give him the kiss of life?' said Dad, giving me a hug too. 'How did you know what to do?'

'I just sort of sussed it out. I didn't do much. I'm not really a hero,' I said, trying to wriggle free of Mum and Dad, scared everyone would start laughing again.

But no-one was laughing now. Prickle-Head was carried up the cliff to be taken to hospital. He seemed reasonably OK now, though he had sick all down his front.

'That Tim rescued you. He gave you the kiss of life,' said Pinch-Face.

'No wonder I was sick!' Prickle-Head gasped.

He wasn't at all grateful! But I didn't care. Everyone kept saying I was a hero. And back at the carnival they gave me a special cup. It was supposed to be for the child that won the most races.

'But *you* must have it instead, Tim!'

'I'm ever so glad you're my boyfriend, Tim,' said Kelly.

'You're a *real* Super-Tim,' said Biscuits.

I don't know about that. I'm not *quite* Super-Tim standard.

But I'm Tim – and I *feel* Super!

THE MUM-MINDER
Jacqueline Wilson

I'm Sadie and I'm nearly nine. Mum's a
childminder, but she doesn't have to mind
me. I can mind myself, easy-peasy. Lucky for
Mum, because now she's got the flu, so I've
got to mind her – and help with all the
babies!

A hilarious, entertaining and lively account,
told throughout in Sadie's own words, of one
chaotic week in the life of a young girl whose
mother is a childminder.

'Funny and warm-hearted'
Daily Mail

0 440 863023

CORGI YEARLING BOOKS

GLUBBSLYME
Jacqueline Wilson

*Glubbslyme settled himself on the bank,
looking up at the sky. His bulbous eyes
protruded until they looked as if they might
pop out altogether. Then they started
revolving . . .*

Glubbslyme is no ordinary huge, black,
warty toad. As Rebecca, his unexpectedly
new found friend discovers, he's hundreds of
years old, can talk and even claims to be
able to work magic!

When Glubbslyme comes to live with
Rebecca, her happy plans are soon turned
upside-down. Will anything work out as she
expects . . .?

0 440 862310

CORGI YEARLING BOOKS

BAD GIRLS
Jacqueline Wilson

*Kim's gang had better watch out!
Because Tanya's my friend now, and she'll
show them*

Mandy has been picked on at school for as
long as she can remember. That's why she is
delighted when cheeky, daring, full-of-fun
Tanya picks her as a friend. Mum isn't
happy – she thinks Tanya's a BAD GIRL and
a bad influence. Mandy's sure Tanya can
only get her out of trouble, not in to it . . . or
could she?

0 440 863562

CORGI YEARLING BOOKS